"I don't know what happened to your wife in Desolation Canyon," Kit said, "but I am not her."

Hawke closed the space between them. Hissing in a breath, Kit went rigid, leaning back so far she could easily topple over the sofa with the slightest movement. Through clenched teeth, he muttered, "Don't you ever bring my wife up again."

Her chin went up another notch. "Oh, I see. It's okay for you to play unfair, but not me."

He thrust his face close to hers. Panic flared in her eyes, but he didn't back down. Too much was at stake. "This isn't a game. Haven't you figured that out yet?"

"You are not my keeper," she said. "My work is very important to me, but I assure you I won't take unnecessary risks."

"So you've hiked in places like Desolation Canyon before?" he asked.

"Well, not exactly. If I had, I wouldn't need you."

Need you. Those words struck terror into his heart.

MARGARET DALEY

feels she has been blessed. She has been married more than thirty years to her husband, Mike, whom she met in college. He is a terrific support and her best friend. They have one son, Shaun. Margaret has been writing for many years and loves to tell a story. When she was a little girl, she would play with her dolls and make up stories about their lives. Now she writes these stories down. She especially enjoys weaving stories about families and how faith in God can sustain a person when things get tough. When she isn't writing, she is fortunate to be a teacher for students with special needs. Margaret has taught for over twenty years and loves working with her students. She has also been a Special Olympics coach and participated in many sports with her students.

MARGARET DALEY

Forsaken Canyon

Steeple Hill®

Published by Steeple Hill Books™

STEEPLE HILL BOOKS

Steeple
Hill®

ISBN-13: 978-0-373-44309-3
ISBN-10:   0-373-44309-9

FORSAKEN CANYON

Blessed is that man that maketh the Lord his trust.
—*Psalms* 40:4

To Terri and Rene, thanks for
all the years of friendship

PROLOGUE

The Guardian wished he hadn't been forced to do this, but someone had to save Kit from her fiancé. She was just too naive and trusting.

Comfortably hidden in the shut-off balcony of the church, he lined up his sights on the rifle and aimed for the man's heart. The sounds of the bridal march reverberated through the large nave. With precision and preparation he would succeed, and one day she would thank him.

Her fiancé stood on the steps to the altar, facing the center aisle. The smile the man gave Kit—as though he really loved her—chilled the Guardian. She deserved so much better.

Calmness descended as he adjusted his grip, checking his target. The sight of her nearing her fiancé prompted him into action. Taking a deep breath, he held it while fingering the trigger.

This is for you, Kit. He squeezed off the shot.

ONE

Kit Sinclair sat bolt upright in bed, darkness pressing in on all sides. Her lungs burned as she dragged air into them. The sound of her heart pounding thundered in her ears like the roar of a powerful storm.

Just another nightmare. I'm safe in my bedroom.

But the thought didn't assuage the terror that constricted her chest as if she were standing in front of the altar right now. She could still see the red stain fanning outward on her fiancé's snowy-white shirt, and Gregory's hand reaching out to her. The screams in the church resounded through her mind. The scent of her fiancé's blood filled her nostrils as though she were still holding his body clutched to her.

Will I ever be free of the memories, Lord?

She raked a wavering hand through her sweat-damp hair, then reached for the lamp on her bedside table. After two failed attempts, she finally managed to pull the chain, and a soft glow flooded the black recesses of her room. But her mind still remained in the clutch of darkness, had since the day her fiancé had been murdered right in front of her two years ago.

Glancing at her clock, she noted the time and realized she'd only gotten a few hours of sleep. She flipped back the sheet and climbed from the bed. She might as well work since she had to get up early anyway to drive from Albuquerque to her meeting in nearby Santa Maria Pueblo this morning.

Thankfully she had something to concentrate on other than her past. She could do nothing about what had happened, but she could prove her theory was right, hopefully with the help of Zach Collier's cousin. If not she would find another way. Her job at the college depended on it.

Hawke Lonechief finished the dregs of his coffee and motioned for Anna, the owner of the café and his cousin, to refill it. "I'm gonna need it this morning."

"Another all-nighter?"

"How can you tell?" Hawke took a tentative sip of the black brew, relishing its strong flavor, just the way he liked it, no sugar, no cream.

"Cousin, we grew up together. I know when you haven't gotten any sleep. Do you ever see your mother?"

"Sure, we had dinner together two nights ago." And his mother had basically read him the riot act, although in her case it was mainly said with her usual few words. She was worried about him. But, for him, working held the haunting memories at bay.

"You're the chief of police, so why are you doing everything down at the station? What are the other officers for?"

Hawk shrugged. "What's wrong with working?"

"Nothing, if in moderation. But you don't know the meaning of the word."

He grinned. "Sure I do. It means steering clear of any excesses. I don't have time for excesses."

"You don't call nearly living at the station an excess?"

She fluttered her hand in the air. "Nope. Don't answer that. I never could change your mind while we were growing up. I don't know why I even waste my breath trying to now."

"I'm responsible for the safety and well-being of thousands of people. I don't take that responsibility lightly."

"And you shouldn't, but what about your mother? Have you left Aunt Evelyn to fend for herself on the ranch?"

Stung by the rebuke of his well-meaning cousin, Hawke straightened in the booth and cupped the mug between his hands while he drank some more coffee. "Charlie's wife got sick. Somebody had to take care of his small children. I couldn't ask him to take his usual shift last night."

Anna wagged her head. "There's always something with you. Go home. Get some sleep." She sent him a quizzical look. "You are going home, aren't you?"

"Yes, I am as soon as I meet with someone. Then home it is."

"Good, because that ranch is too much for Aunt Evelyn alone."

"That's why I hired some more help."

"Who?"

"Lighthorse's oldest son, John."

"Good. He's reliable. She needs someone who is."

"Ouch." The persistent reproach in Anna's voice needled Hawke. "As I told you, I have responsibilities I can't shirk."

"I know and we appreciate it. Crime is down at the pueblo since you took over as police chief. But we both know what this is really about."

The door to the café opened, and a petite woman with long blond hair tied back in a ponytail entered. Hawke zeroed in on her, rather than continue the conversation, because there was no way he would get into a discussion with Anna about *that*.

The attractive woman scanned the tables and booths until she found him and then immediately headed in his direction. As he watched her move with assurance and economy, alarm bells—bells he usually listened to—went off in his mind. What had possessed him to agree to meet with this woman? He should have told his cousin Zach no.

Behind the pleasing features, he glimpsed a woman on a mission. The determined set to her chin and the focused look in her blue eyes alerted him to be wary. He didn't need trouble. He'd had enough of that to last him two lifetimes.

Exhausted from no sleep in twenty-four hours, Hawke tried to paste a semblance of a smile on his face in greeting. Once he made a commitment, he didn't back out no matter how much he wanted to. The corners of his mouth twitched in protest. He gave up and rose instead.

"Dr. Kit Sinclair?"

"Yes. You must be Zach's cousin, Hawke Lonechief." She grinned and took his hand to shake.

The brief, firm exchange didn't relieve the tension building in his gut. He waved his arm toward the seat across from him. "Please, sit."

After she slipped into the booth, Anna, who had been hovering on the side observing the meeting with more interest than Hawke would like, approached. "What can I get for you?"

"I've heard great things about your coffee here at the café from Zach Collier. That's all I need." *That and the man across from me to agree to be my guide to Desolation Canyon.*

"You know Zach?"

"I'm a professor of history at Albuquerque City College. We have worked together on a few projects."

"Science and history working together?" The waitress poured a mug full of the wonderfully fragrant coffee.

"Thank you." Kit lifted the cup to her mouth and drew in a deep breath of the aroma, one of the best smells in the world, especially since she tried to avoid sleeping as much as possible. She could use the whole pot after last night. "I helped Zach with some of the history behind his Aztec codices, at least the part that involved the Spanish conquistadors. That's one of my specialties."

Normally she wouldn't go into so much detail except that she wanted the man across from her to know the information. Zach had told her Hawke Lonechief was the best person to help her, possibly the only one. He knew every square foot of Santa Maria Pueblo, and he could survive where most people couldn't. The place she wanted to go to wasn't called Desolation Canyon without reason. It was a hard, rough, barren land.

Like your life. The thought came unbidden into her mind. She shoved it away.

After the waitress left, Kit lounged back against the cushion, trying to relax her taut muscles. Even running through the mental relaxation technique a friend had taught her did nothing to alleviate the stress mounting in her as she got closer to discovering if her theory was right or not. Nor was imagining herself on top of a mountain, looking out over a beautiful vista right before the sun went down doing the trick—not when dark-brown eyes studied her with an intensity that stole her breath, her composure.

She did her own survey of the man. He was dressed in tan slacks and shirt with an emblem indicating he was a tribal police officer. His short black hair surprised her. She had pictured him with long hair on the hour drive from Albuquerque. What else would surprise her?

"Now that we have finished sizing each other up, why do you need a guide? Zach didn't tell me much. Just that you two worked together and you were a friend." Hawke finished his coffee and set it on the table.

Direct. She liked that. "I'm looking for evidence of the Lost City of Gold."

"Who isn't? But at Santa Maria Pueblo? I don't think so."

The territorial tone of his voice warned her this might not be an easy sell. "I think there was a lot of truth to the legend that sent Coronado all over the Southwest looking for it. Working with Zach, and what I discovered while in Spain researching the topic for my dissertation, has only reinforced my conviction, which has grown the past several years."

One corner of Hawke's mouth hitched up. "Sure. Who wouldn't want to find a place so full of gold that all your worries would be taken care of."

She stiffened at his mocking tone, but she realized that after all this time the tale did sound far-fetched. "I think there was a place that prompted the legend, but I'm not saying it exists today as it did five hundred years ago or that it was as grand as the story said. If it did, it probably would have been discovered."

He folded his arms on the table and leaned forward. "Do you make it a habit to go around telling people you're looking for the Lost City of Gold?"

"No," she said with a chuckle. "They would think I was mad."

"Are you?"

"No. Sorry to disappoint you. I'm perfectly sane. But I need a guide, and Zach said you were the best, that you helped him and Maggie last year with the Aztec codices. I trust Zach's opinion."

"So you trust me?"

"Yes." Did she have a choice?

"You shouldn't." His almost-black gaze drilled into her. "If there is a City of Gold out there and you're looking for it, I wouldn't trust anyone. People do a lot of nasty things for money."

"To put your mind at rest, I haven't advertised the fact in the Albuquerque newspaper."

"That's comforting, because after what Zach, Maggie and I, to a lesser degree, went through last year because of the codices, I would hate to see that happen to you."

She inclined her head. "I'm touched by your concern."

"If something happened to you at Santa Maria Pueblo, I would have to deal with it. *That's* my job, not being a tour guide."

His use of the word *tour* stung Kit. "I wouldn't require much of your time. And, of course, I would pay for that time. I estimate five or six days to confirm if the remains of the Spanish mission are what I'm looking for."

For a few seconds any emotion in his expression disappeared. Then a relentlessness scored his features. Tension vibrated in the air as he drew himself up, his large presence commanding. "Where do you expect to find these ruins?"

"The ruins are the ones you found a few years ago in Desolation Canyon. Zach told me about it a month ago when we were working on some background information for the new exhibit at the museum." As she spoke, his expression turned to fury, as though a storm had swept into the café. This didn't bode well for what she wanted. "Can you give me a few days of your—"

"No. I can't." He surged to his feet and tossed down some dollars. "Goodbye, Dr. Sinclair."

As he stalked to the exit, Kit held her hands over the lukewarm coffee, trying to draw any warmth she could from it, because the temperature in the restaurant had definitely dropped twenty degrees in the past minute.

Desolation Canyon was in such a remote part of the reservation that few people visited there, and not usually because they wanted to. But why had he reacted like that? Did he know something about the canyon she didn't?

Making a quick decision, she hurriedly paid for her drink and followed him outside. She had to know what she was getting into, because if he wouldn't guide her, she would have to find someone who would. This was too important and could be a huge boost to her career.

Kit caught him scrambling into his Jeep. "Mr. Lonechief," she called out from across the small parking lot on the side of the café.

He glanced at her and slammed his door shut. The next thing she heard was the roar of the engine. Brazenly she shot out in front of his vehicle before he put it into Drive, and blocked his path. He scowled as she came around to his window, her hand at all times on his Jeep as if she would cling to it if he sped away.

"What's the problem with Desolation Canyon?"

He quirked an eyebrow. "Besides being isolated, ruggedly harsh and not the latest tourist destination?"

"I know it won't be an easy hike. But there's something you aren't telling me."

He firmed his mouth into an even deeper frown. "Stay away from there."

"Why?" She leaned toward him, her hands braced against his door.

A nerve in his jaw jerked. He stared forward for the longest moment, then muttered, "My wife died in that canyon. Now if you'll excuse me, Dr. Sinclair, I've been up all night and need some sleep." Hawke pointedly peered at her hands still on his Jeep door.

His revelation stunned her. It took a few seconds for a question to form in her mind. "How? What happened?"

Anger hardened his clenched jaw. He revved his engine.

"Will you at least recommend another guide?"

His expression blanked, leaving no indication of what he was thinking or feeling. "No."

"You can't be the only guide available!" She stepped back, because the scorch of his look convinced her not to try to stop him from leaving. She was only brave to a point.

"Stay away from there." Hawke threw the black Jeep into Drive and screeched out of the parking lot.

Weary, she closed her eyes for a few seconds. When she opened them, his vehicle had vanished from her view. He must have broken a few laws getting away from her. If she weren't so desperate for help, she would laugh about what just happened or cry at his revelation. But a couple of years ago she had determined emotions wouldn't rule her life—ever again.

Her career was everything to her now. She was a researcher, more at home in a library surrounded by books, delving into the mysteries of the past. She couldn't believe she had actually stood in front of his car to stop him from leaving. *Woman of action* had never been a description of her.

* * *

The lines and words on the map blurred together. Kit rubbed her eyes, but still her vision protested the hours spent researching in the college library. She wanted to make sure she knew all the history of Desolation Canyon and the best way into it. What she needed was a map with little dotted lines that led to the Spanish mission. The church was the key to the whereabouts of the City of Gold.

"Why am I not surprised to find you buried under a stack of books?" Dr. Zach Collier of the science department picked up a thick tome and read its title. "My, such a heavy topic about the climate conditions in the 1500s at such an early hour."

"History of an area or time is more than people."

"I imagine climate can have a huge impact on what happens through history. So how did the meeting with Hawke go yesterday?"

She frowned. "Not too well. He won't be my guide."

"I was afraid of that." Zach slid into the chair across from her.

"Why didn't you tell me his wife died in that canyon?"

Surprise widened Zach's eyes. "He told you?"

"Yes. He didn't know how else to get rid of me. What happened?"

"I don't know much. I wasn't living here at the time, and he won't talk about it to anyone. Not even Evelyn will say anything. All I know is that it happened four years ago while he was home visiting his mother with his wife, Pamela."

"Visiting? I thought he'd always lived here."

"No. He went to college and law school at Yale. After he married Pamela, he became a junior partner in her father's law firm in New York City. They came to New Mexico for a vacation, and on one of their hiking trips into the canyons northwest of here, Pamela fell from a cliff. Hawke only went back to New York to pack up his things."

"It would have been helpful if I'd known that before I approached him." Kit closed the volume she'd been studying.

"I was hoping it wouldn't make a difference to Hawke. I thought the mention of the Lost City of Gold would prick his interest."

"No, more like his derision."

"Since the accident he hasn't been the same. Evelyn doesn't say much about it, but I know she's worried about her son."

"And you're worried about him, too?"

"Yes, and he won't let me help. He's turned away from the Lord."

"It's sad how some people feel they have to wade through their problems by themselves. No one has to do that." She remembered in the parking lot, before he'd driven away, the glimpse of hurt in his dark eyes that she instinctively knew he would deny.

"The Lord is always there for a person if he or she will only turn to Him."

"True, and something I'm glad I've done." Kit checked her watch. "I have a class in an hour and still have to look over my notes." Rising, she gathered up the books before her.

Zach came to his feet. "What are you going to do now about going to the canyon?"

"Find another guide. Because after looking over a map of the area, I know I can't do it alone. You wouldn't happen to know anyone else who could do the job?"

"Not like Hawke. Sorry."

"I'll find someone. I'm not going to let this stop me."

"I didn't think it would, but be careful. That's rough, isolated country."

"First your cousin warns me and now you. It's just another canyon, not some evil place."

"I agree places aren't evil, but people are. Be careful who you tell you're looking for the Lost City of Gold. With Hawke you can be up front, but with others you shouldn't."

Kit chuckled. "Zach Collier, I appreciate your concern, but I've been on my own now for a while. I know how to take care of myself." She'd had to learn how to do that because there was no way she would ever become involved with another man. After Gregory's murder, she'd decided she would have to be satisfied with being single. That was when she had come to the conclusion her career would be her life.

He raised his hands, palms out. "My wife would be furious if I didn't warn you."

"Tell Maggie hi for me, and let her know I'll call her soon. See you." She carried the stack of books to the counter.

"Kit, did you find everything you were looking for today?" Samuel White, the research librarian who was always such a big help to her, pushed the books to the side.

"Yes and no. There's a part missing, but I haven't figured out what yet. Just as soon as I do, I'll have you do a search for me in the network. I know we don't have it here."

"Just let me know, and I'll find what you need."

"Thanks."

Another quick glance at her watch told her she would be late if she didn't hurry. However, outside she couldn't resist pausing for a few seconds and scanning the campus. A beautiful day. The bright sunlight lifted her spirits after the conversation with Zach, as though the Lord had orchestrated it just for her.

Multicolored flowers bloomed in the gardens that greeted the students as they entered the library. Tall maple trees lined the long walk that led to its main entrance, offering a person a cool reprieve from the heat. She wished she had time to enjoy the perfect spring day, but she quickly headed toward the history building, not far from the library.

Zach hadn't given her much hope of convincing Hawke to be her guide, so she was left with only one option: to find another one. After class she had some thinking and planning to do.

When she arrived at her office, she found Dr. Wes Stanford waiting by her door. "Good morning."

He smiled, his white teeth standing out against his tanned face. "I saw you from my window coming into the building. I thought this would be a good time for me to get that article you wanted me to read."

"Let me find it." She unlocked her door and entered. "I brought it from home a few days ago after we talked about it." She rummaged through the piles on her desk and discovered the copy at the bottom of one of them.

"I'm always amazed at your resources." Wes took it from her outstretched hand.

Shrugging, she stepped back to allow more space between them. "I love researching and collect everything I can get my hands on that has to do with history, especially early-American history, before we were a country."

"I'd like to take you to lunch as a way of thanking you for all your help. How about after your ten-o'clock class today?"

"You don't have to do that, Wes. I'm glad to help you any

way I can." She leaned back against her desk, aware of her notes that she wanted to read over sitting behind her just waiting for her. But Wes was a friend and the newest history professor on staff. "After all, I've got a vested interest in your career since I was your graduate advisor. It's good to see how well you're doing."

"After that, I think I should scratch lunch plans and take you to dinner instead." Wes moved closer.

Sweat glazed her forehead and upper lip. He'd invaded her personal space, although there was at least a foot between them. But with the desk behind her, she had little room to maneuver away. She offered him a trembling smile. "I wish I could, but I'm swamped right now. Maybe another time."

"Sure." He backed up, his grin wavering for a few seconds before he reinforced it.

Kit inhaled a deep breath and relaxed her grip on the edge of her desk. When he left, she slipped into the chair nearby, her legs weak. Why hadn't she seen his interest before? Maybe she was jumping to the wrong conclusion, and it was only appreciation for what she'd helped him with during the three years of their close association, first as a graduate student and now as a professor.

She liked Wes; she saw the same appreciation for history as she had, but that was all she would ever feel toward any man—friendship. Discovering Gregory's betrayal on top of dealing with his murder had nearly sent her over the edge. The Lord and her friends had managed to hold her together, but she didn't want to go through that kind of loss ever again.

She caught sight of her notes on her desk and stood. She still needed to reread them before her class. Afterward, she would tackle the problem of finding a guide.

* * *

A bright shaft of light slanted across Hawke's desk at the police station. He finished the report and slapped the folder closed. Time to go home. He needed to check and see if his new ranch hand was working out. Anna was right, not that he would ever tell her. He should pay more attention to the family ranch and make sure his mother wasn't burdened with too much work.

He started to rise from his chair, but the phone ringing stopped him in midaction. He sank back down and snatched up the receiver. "Lonechief."

"Hawke—"

He instantly recognized Zach's voice and sat up straight, remembering whom his cousin had sent to him only a couple of days ago.

"Maggie and I want you to come to dinner at our house before the dedication of the Collier/Somers Wing of the museum."

"I forgot about the dedication. It's this Saturday night?"

"Yes, in just two days. I'm glad I called to remind you. Is Evelyn coming?"

"She wouldn't miss it for the world, but Albert is bringing her."

"Albert Cloudwalker? Doesn't he own the trading post by the highway into Albuquerque?"

"Yes, and yes, Mama has been seeing him."

"Interesting."

There was a wealth of questions in that one word. "I'm glad she's seeing someone finally."

A long pause, then, "I wish you would reconsider taking Kit to Desolation Canyon."

Hawke had known that Zach would approach him about

this, but it didn't make any difference. He wouldn't go to the canyon again. He couldn't. Not there. "What time is dinner?"

"Six, since the dedication ceremony is at eight. And I get the point. No more talking about Kit and Desolation Canyon."

"I've always said you were the smart one in the family, that is, after your grandfather."

"I take that as a compliment. Red was exceptional."

"See you Saturday." Hawke hung up, staring at the pool of sunlight warming his desk.

A picture of a no-nonsense woman with long blond hair and blue eyes materialized in his mind. The determination he'd glimpsed in her worried him. He wouldn't put it past her to try to find someone else to take her into the canyon. The only other person capable of doing that was his uncle. Thankfully Gus lived halfway between here and the canyon, and he rarely came into town. Even if he did, Hawke wasn't concerned Gus would agree to guide the professor into that maze of ravines and mesas. His uncle was a hermit and hated to be around people. Gus only tolerated Hawke for short periods of time because he took him his supplies every couple of months. But everything he'd learned about the land was from his uncle.

Tired, Hawke flattened his hands on his desktop and pushed himself to his feet. Even if she tried to find someone, she wouldn't.

He headed toward the door and left the station before something came up to keep him there. Yes, he worked a lot of hours, but he knew when he needed to sleep. With long strides he covered the distance to his Jeep quickly and climbed inside.

As he pulled out of the parking space in front of the tribal police station, he peered both ways down the lengthy street that ran through the heart of the small town of San Angelo. His gaze lit upon a woman coming out of Anna's café, and he braked. He watched Dr. Kit Sinclair stroll toward the red Honda parked in front.

Almost as though his arms and legs had a mind of their own, he made a U-turn and drove toward the café.

TWO

I'm doing my job by discovering what she's up to. If she does something foolish, I'm the one who will have to clean up the mess.

Yeah, right, nothing else motivates you.

Hawke ignored that little voice in his head and came to a halt a few feet from her car. The woman he wished he could ban from the pueblo wheeled around, her eyes growing round as he slipped from his Jeep.

"I didn't think I would see you again in San Angelo." He hadn't intended to fling a challenge in her face, but somehow his words came out that way.

She stiffened, a white-knuckled grip on her black purse straps. "I didn't think I had to ask your permission."

"What brings you out this way a second time?"

She pinched her lips together and opened her car door. "Nothing that concerns you. Now, if you don't mind, I need to get back to town."

He observed her driving away and decided to do a little investigating. Striding to the café's entrance, he knew if anyone could tell him why Kit was in town it would be Anna.

Inside, only a few tables held customers enjoying a late

lunch. He scanned the large room and saw his cousin behind the counter, talking with Lester Running Bear, his long black hair hanging in a braid down his back. As Hawke moved toward Anna, the older man rose and turned toward him. A frown marred his craggy face.

"See ya, Anna." Avoiding the direct path to the exit, his head down, Lester circumvented Hawke.

Hawke stopped at the long counter that ran the length of the café. "Has Lester been drinking? Is that why he's dodging me?"

"He was sober." Anna began wiping down the laminated top, her gaze averted.

"What aren't you telling me?" Hawke settled onto a stool.

She stopped her cleaning and looked him directly in the eye. "Lester's going to be Kit Sinclair's guide to Desolation Canyon."

He leaped to his feet and started for the door, then realized that the woman in question was probably halfway to the highway to Albuquerque. He came back to Anna. "Why didn't you try to stop that?"

"Because I didn't know until after she left. Lester was just telling me."

"He can't do that. He's never sober long enough to show anyone anything."

"Then I suggest you give her a call and tell her that."

After the look she'd sent him out in the parking lot, he was sure that the second he identified himself she would slam down the phone. He would be in Albuquerque in two days for the dedication ceremony. He'd go see her then and make her listen to him. There was no way he would let Lester guide her anywhere.

* * *

Saturday evening Hawke rang Kit Sinclair's bell. When no one answered, he pounded on the door. After a few minutes, he had to acknowledge she wasn't home, which meant he would now have to make an extra trip into town to see her. Unless she was at the dedication tonight for the Collier/Somers Wing at the museum. She'd helped Zach with the exhibit, so hopefully Hawke would see her there and set her straight.

Leaving the porch, he headed toward his Jeep in the driveway. If she wasn't at the museum, he would stop by on the way back to the pueblo. He didn't intend to stay late at the ceremony, anyway.

"She's already left," said the distinguished-looking neighbor. Probably in his early forties, he held a hose, watering his plants, most of them cacti, along the border of his property with Kit's.

"Do you know if she'll be back soon?" He could be a little late to Zach's if it would save him a trip into Albuquerque another day.

The man removed his hat, revealing thick, wavy blond hair. "I don't think so. She said something about a function at the college. I can tell her you came by, Mr...."

Hawke took the man's outstretched hand and shook it. "Hawke Lonechief. I don't think that'll be necessary. We're going to the same function. I'll catch her there." At least, he hoped they were, and he could put an end to the woman's pipe dream once and for all. He definitely was going to have a word with Zach about putting such a foolish idea into Kit's head.

Since his cousin lived across town from Kit's, Hawke had

some time to plot his strategy. He really had no way of stopping anyone from going into that maze of canyons if that person was determined—like Kit—but he was sure going to try with her. He wondered if she even owned a pair of hiking boots. She had *amateur* written all over her face. Even if he hadn't known exactly the hazards of the tangle of sheer cliffs, pockmarked land, treacherous escarpments that led to Desolation, not to mention the dangers in the canyon itself, he still would have discouraged her.

He wished he'd discouraged Pamela. But his wife had wanted an adventure—something risky and challenging. And he'd agreed, wanting to please her after the fight they'd had about living in New York City.

If only he had remembered what Gus had said about the canyon, with its blood-red walls when the sunlight struck it just right. If only—

Hawke shoved the thought from his mind, along with the vision of his wife the last moment he'd seen her alive. Her smile would haunt him forever. As would her scream as she plunged down to the bottom of the jagged, rocky ravine below.

Twenty minutes later he pulled in front of Zach's house and noticed the red Honda sitting in the driveway. For a few seconds he considered leaving and grabbing dinner somewhere else before the ceremony. But he'd never run from a problem before, and this would be a good time to have that little conversation with the good professor.

His long strides quickly chewed up the space between his Jeep and the porch. When Zach opened the front door to his knock, Hawke entered, surveying the entry hall and spacious room off to the side.

"Where is she?" Hawke asked, stopping in the middle of the living area.

"Who?"

Amusement flickered in Zach's eyes, producing a swell of anger in Hawke. "You know good and well who I'm talking about. Kit Sinclair."

"I'm right here."

The voice, husky for a woman, sounded behind him. Hawke pivoted toward her. She stood just inside the living room with a brown leather couch between them. "We need to talk about Lester Running Bear."

"I'll leave you two alone." Zach hurried toward the French doors that led out onto the deck.

"No, we don't," Kit said when the click of the door closing announced they were by themselves. "Lester has agreed to be my guide. You wouldn't, so it's none of your business."

"It's my business when you're engaging a man who is rarely sober for longer than a day and can't find his way out of a building with a well-lit exit sign."

Blinking, she looked away. When she reestablished eye contact with him, her neutral expression hid her earlier surprise. "You gave up that right when you turned me down."

"Have you talked to Lester today?"

"What have you done?" She covered the few feet to the sofa and grasped its back.

"Convinced him not to take you."

Glaring at him, Kit opened her mouth but snapped it closed before saying anything. She sucked in a soothing breath. "Do you make it a practice to interfere with some-one's life like that?"

"Yes, when that someone ignores my advice." He circled behind the sofa and stopped just two feet short of her.

Kit plastered herself against the back of the couch, her gaze flittering from one side of him to the other. "I don't know what you think you're doing, but I'm going to that canyon with or without your help."

"Lady, there is no one else, so make it easy on yourself and give the idea up."

"You mean make it easy on you." Lifting her chin, she stabbed him with a withering look. "I'll find someone else, and if not, then I'll go by myself."

"Then I'll arrest you."

"On what grounds?"

"Jaywalking. I'll come up with something."

"I don't know what happened to your wife in Desolation Canyon, but I am not her."

He closed the space between them. Hissing in a breath, Kit went rigid, leaning back so far she could easily topple over the sofa with the slightest movement. Through clenched teeth, he muttered, "Don't you ever bring my wife up again."

Her chin went up another notch. "Oh, I see. It's okay if you play unfair, but not me."

He thrust his face close to hers. Panic flared in her eyes, but he didn't back down. Too much was at stake. "This isn't a game. Haven't you figured that out yet?"

She brought her hands up and fisted them against his chest, then shoved him back a few feet. Scurrying to the side, she rounded the couch. "I'm very aware of the stakes. My career is on the line."

"So you would risk your life for your career?"

"Life is a risk." She shrugged, all the earlier tension evaporating. "What if you and Zach hadn't taken a chance last year? You all would never have found the Aztec codices. He can write his own ticket anywhere now because of that discovery."

Her words threw him back four years to his last argument with Pamela. She'd practically said that very same thing to him. She'd wanted him to take a big corporate fraud case that he'd wanted nothing to do with. In fact, he'd brought her to New Mexico in the hopes of convincing her to relocate here. If they had stayed in New York, she would be alive today. He would have to live with that the rest of his life.

"This isn't about Zach or me. It's about you." Balling his hands at his sides, he fought to keep his temper in check, but it boiled in his stomach.

"You are *not* my keeper. My work is very important to me, but I assure you I won't take unnecessary risks."

There was nothing reassuring about what she said. His gut twisted into a huge knot. "Do you even know what an unnecessary risk is?"

"I'm a highly educated woman. I've lived in New Mexico for half my life." She pulled herself up tall.

"So you've hiked in places like Desolation Canyon?"

"Well, not exactly. If I had, I wouldn't need you."

Need you. Those words stuck terror into his heart. "Where have you hiked?"

"In Chaco, Mesa Verde."

He choked back a laugh. "I can see you are prepared."

Her glare returned. "I'll do what it takes to be prepared. Now if you'll excuse me, I'm suddenly not hungry. I'm sure you can explain to Zach and Maggie why I left early."

The slamming of the front door echoed through Zach's house and brought his cousin inside.

"Obviously, the discussion didn't go as I had planned."

Hawke rounded on Zach. "What did you think I was going to do? I don't back down. You know that."

"You do when you're wrong."

"You think I am?"

"The information she has gathered is good. There just might be a Lost City of Gold out there or some other significant archaeological find."

"Then you take her."

"I would if I knew the area like you and hadn't already committed to an expedition this summer. Besides, I'm not a real archaeologist."

"You're the best amateur I've seen. And don't forget you're used to fieldwork as an anthropologist."

"This is probably a piece of cake after our adventure last year. At least there are no people trying to kill her and get the information she has."

"If she keeps going around telling people about it, there will be." Hawke curled his hands into fists, remembering vividly how close he, Zach and Maggie had come to dying last year. He'd never been concerned about his own life, just his cousin's and Maggie's.

"She's smart. She knows when to keep her mouth shut."

"What's for dinner? I'm starved."

Chuckling, Zach threw his arms up in the air. "I won't mention it again—tonight. Let's go eat."

Kit stormed up to her porch and plopped down on the glider where she always liked to sit and work out her problems. The Guardian had been surprised when his GPS tracking device he'd planted under her car had indicated she was returning home. She hadn't been gone long.

Even in the dimming light, he could see her face clearly through the binoculars. Someone had made her angry. Who? The man who had come to her house earlier that evening. He'd left clearly displeased. Had he found Kit? Had he upset her?

He would have to find out what was going on with her. He didn't like her unhappy. Whatever it was, he could fix it. Although it was getting harder, years ago he had made it his purpose in life to protect her and give her what she needed. After all, he owed her.

It was a shame, though; sometimes she didn't know what was best for her.

But that's why I'm here.

The following week the door to Hawke's office crashed open. Kit filled the entrance in all her anger. She stormed toward him as if a tornado swept through the station and planted her fists on his desk, leaning across it.

"What gives you the right to ruin my life?"

He met her fury with calm, folding his hands on his calendar blotter with his fingers interlaced. "I thought we had this little discussion last Saturday at Zach's."

"This isn't about Lester."

"Then what's it about?"

"I hired James Harrison to be my guide, and now he has disappeared. No one has seen him. What did you do to make him leave town?"

"Who is James Harrison? I don't know anyone by that name at Santa Maria Pueblo."

"After Lester, I got smart. I looked elsewhere for my

guide. So how did you find out about Mr. Harrison? I didn't even say anything to Zach in case he let it slip to you."

"Where in the world did you find this Harrison?"

She straightened, waving her hand in the air. "That's not important. He lives in the area."

"He does? At the pueblo?"

"Well, no. Albuquerque. He assured me he knew what he was doing. He had references."

"Ah, references are important." Why hadn't he noticed how cute she was when she was angry? Her full lips formed a perfect little pout, and her eyes sparked with blue fire. But she was definitely trouble. He had to remember that.

"They are. He's led several groups through various canyons in the state."

"Any to Desolation Canyon?"

"No, but isn't one canyon like another?"

"No, not at all." Hawke lounged back in his comfortably padded chair. The day had turned interesting after a rather dull start. "And if you have to ask me that, then you have no business going in there."

"You're just saying that to keep me away." She sank into the seat across from his desk.

"To put your mind at rest, I did not say anything to Harrison because I didn't know about him." His elbows on the arms of his chair, he steepled his fingers. "Contrary to what you may be thinking, I've not been following you around to see who you'll contact next. I'll tell you, however, that I've let it be known I wouldn't be too happy if someone from the pueblo was your guide."

"I don't give up easily, especially now." Her eyes narrowed.

He knew he shouldn't ask, but he did. "Especially now?"

"I discovered some more collaborating evidence that I'm on the right track."

"What?"

"Zach gave me a piece of advice I think I'll take. Trust no one."

Hawke laughed. "That sounds like my cousin. And in this situation I have to agree. Although I don't think there's a City of Gold out there, just the mere mention of the word *gold* makes men do crazy things."

"That's it." She leaped from the chair, her features red with anger. "You're going after it without me." She stretched her upper body across his desk as if she were coming at him. "You won't find it without my information."

"Aren't you forgetting that I'm the one who discovered the ruins of the mission? Do you know where they are?"

She settled back, a scowl slashing across her face. "In Desolation Canyon."

"It covers a lot of ground. Give it up, Dr. Sinclair. You have no business going there. You're out of shape and in no condition to make the trek." After picking up the folder closest to him, he flipped it open. "You may have time to travel all the way here on a whim, but I have work to do and don't have any more time to chitchat."

Kit wanted to bang her hands on the desk to get his attention as he perused the papers in the folder. His nonchalant bearing conveyed he had not a care in the world. She wouldn't bang his desk, but she would find a way around the man. He blocked her path to what she wanted. She'd found James Harrison, so she would come up with another escort, and this time she wouldn't say anything to anyone, not even her neighbor who was her sounding board.

After a few seconds of staring at the top of his head, she

gathered her composure, calm beginning to seep back into her. "Thank *you*, Mr. Lonechief."

Outside in the bright, cloudless day, she examined the small town of San Angelo. Only twenty miles to the north lay the start of the canyon system that led to the place she wanted to go. She'd worked too hard on this theory to back down. She didn't want the gold; she wanted the credit. She had to publish something this year if she was to stay on the faculty at Albuquerque City College and get her tenure. The history department chairperson had made that clear to her, especially in the wake of budget cuts. Her job was all she had now. Yes, she had friends, family and the Lord, but she needed something to do to keep the past at bay, to keep her mind focused forward.

Later that day Kit stared down at the chart showing one-third of New Mexico. "Samuel, I could hug you! This is just what I needed. Where did you get such a detailed map of the area I'm interested in? I've never seen one like this."

"From the archaeology archives."

"I've seen some of their maps, but nothing like this."

He bent toward her and whispered, "These aren't common knowledge and are usually kept under lock and key on the top floor of the library. Even what they are cataloged under doesn't tell anyone much. You see where all the Indian ruins are marked. They don't want people thinking they can go dig them up."

"I know that. Zach told me they keep most of the discovered ruins as is, not excavated. To disturb them would cause more damage and lost knowledge. This will really help."

"Have you found a guide yet?"

"I'm working on it. I've got a lead. No one as skilled as

Zach Collier's cousin, but this map will help make up for the fact I can't get him."

"I need to get it back upstairs. I'll make a copy of it. Just wait right here." Samuel took the map and turned toward the back room behind the counter.

Kit stopped him with a hand on his arm. "You won't get into trouble for bringing the map down here, will you?"

He smiled. "Jessica, who runs that floor, owes me a favor. She knows I have it, but I promised I would bring it back by four, that all I needed to do was check a reference for one of the professors in the archaeology department."

Her hand slipping from his arm, she watched Samuel rush away. She certainly wouldn't be excavating any ruins that had already been discovered, since what she was looking for hadn't been unearthed. Besides, she wasn't an archaeologist. When she found the City of Gold, she would leave that part to the experts.

"It's in there." When Samuel came back, he handed her a large manila envelope. "I had to copy it in sections because of its size."

She took it, so thankful for his assistance. "I'm going to give you that hug." She quickly did. "Thanks again. I've got someone I have to meet upstairs. See you," she said, then hurried toward the steps that led to the third floor.

On the staircase she passed Wes carrying a couple of large volumes. When he came to a stop, she did, too.

"I'm beginning to think you live here," he said with a nervous laugh.

"I've been working on a paper for the American Historical Society magazine." Which was true because she intended to publish her article in it.

"Ah, our publish-or-perish requirement. I've been contemplating what I'll write about. If you've got time later, I would like to discuss it with you."

"You aren't worried I'll steal your idea?"

"Not you." Appreciation glinted in his eyes. "You're the most ethical person I know. Besides, it sounds like you've got yours well under control. Will you be in your office later?"

"No, I'm going home in a few minutes. Come by tomorrow."

"Tomorrow it is." Wes continued his descent to the second floor.

Kit watched him for a few seconds before mounting the steps. She had a meeting with another guide prospect in the back part of the library. Not many people frequented that area, especially during the day. She felt like a spy, setting up a rendezvous, having to consider where she could go without being unduly noticed. Since she was often at the library, no one would think that was strange. Having Ronald Hoffman come to her office was out of the question. The same for her house. So this was it, because she was determined *no one* would know whom she had hired this time.

A tall, thin man removed a book from a shelf and flipped through it before putting it back. He took another one down.

After scanning the area for anyone else, she hastened forward. "Are you Mr. Hoffman?"

He looked toward her. "Yes. Dr. Sinclair?"

She nodded.

"Did you bring the deposit?"

She rummaged in her purse until she found the envelope with the money in it. "You'll get twice that when we complete the trip."

He counted the bills. "I don't know why you want to go

there, but I'll take you for the agreed-upon amount. From what I've heard, it won't be easy." His pinpoint gaze skimmed down her length. "Are you sure you can handle it?"

"Of course. Are you sure you know how to get to Desolation Canyon?"

"Of course. As I told you earlier on the phone, I haven't been there personally, but I know where it is, and that type of terrain is something I'm used to."

"When can we leave?" She hugged the manila envelope to her chest. If he didn't know how to get there, she could figure it out with this detailed map.

"You said something about this Saturday. I can go then." He presented her with a list of supplies. "You'll need to bring these."

"Where do we meet?"

"At Black Horse Pass at seven in the morning. It'll probably take at least five days." He moved past her toward the exit.

"Thank you," she said, but the man had already disappeared around the corner.

Suddenly her legs gave away. She sagged to the floor. What had she set in motion? Ronald Hoffman's credentials had checked out. He'd used to work for an adventure group who had taken people on trips into the wilderness around New Mexico and the surrounding states. If she couldn't have Hawke Lonechief, he was the next best thing.

Kit finished loading her red Honda. The darkness of predawn had lightened to a dim gray, but the sun was still hidden below the eastern horizon. Excitement surged through her at the idea she would be hiking toward Desolation Canyon in a couple of hours.

Marcus Perry, dressed in his navy-blue jogging shorts and white T-shirt, came out onto his porch. She waved at her neighbor and friend. He loped toward her while pulling neon-orange sweatbands on his wrists. From the curious gleam in his eyes, she knew she wouldn't be able to get away without telling him something.

He glanced into her backseat. "Going camping in a certain canyon?"

"I hope. But don't say anything to anyone. You know what happened to the last guide I had."

"So Hawke Lonechief finally agreed."

"No. He still refuses, but this person should be good."

"Who'd you get this time?" Marcus began some limbering-up exercises.

"Ronald Hoffman." Even if Marcus ran into his house right now—which she didn't see her friend doing—it was too late for Hawke to interfere. "He was in the news a few weeks ago. He found that family missing in the Carson National Forest."

"Yeah, I remember reading about him. But the big question is, does he know where you want to go?" Marcus touched his toes.

"He hasn't actually been there, but he's very experienced at being a guide."

"Did I tell you I met him last Saturday night?"

"Who? Ronald?"

"No, Lonechief." He lunged to each side. "Can't be too careful."

"I agree. That's why I checked this Ronald out and no one knows about what I'm doing today."

"Well, except me. But I wasn't talking about your guide. I was talking about exercising. It's so easy to pull a muscle, especially if you don't limber up correctly." He jogged in place. "I think I'm finally loosened up to start my run."

"That's good, but what do you mean you saw Lonechief Saturday night? Did you go to the dedication ceremony?"

"No, he came by here looking for you."

"He did?"

"I caught him pounding on your front door, not too happy you weren't home."

A picture of Hawke frustrated as he stalked back to his Jeep darted through her mind. Good! It served him right for scaring off her other guides. What if at this very moment he was hiking to the canyon to see if what she theorized was true? Now that she thought about it, just because he was Zach's cousin didn't mean she could trust him.

Trust No One. That needed to be her new motto.

"I'd better go. I don't want to be late."

"Before you start hiking, make sure you limber up. I don't want you to pull a muscle out there." Marcus bent forward and kissed her on the cheek.

She slid into her front seat and waved at her friend as he jogged down the street. When she backed out of her driveway, she couldn't stop the feeling of urgency that overcame her. She navigated her car toward the highway that led out of town.

Gold will make men do crazy things. Hawke's words blared through her mind as she drove toward Black Horse Pass. Was Hawke one of those men who did crazy things because of money? When she really thought about everything, what did she know about Zach, who had recommended Hawke in the first place? Her past record where men were concerned wasn't good. She'd had several serious relationships over the years. None spoke well of her ability to choose a man to spend the rest of her life with, especially the last two.

The man she'd been serious with before Gregory only reinforced her conviction to stay away from serious relationships. Terry's reckless driving while under the influence had caused a wreck that had injured a couple. This from a man who had condemned drinking of any kind. He had known how much she hated alcohol and why. What else had he been lying about? Certainly his protestations that he'd only had one drink at the bar. His blood alcohol had been way over the legal limit.

She'd hoped they would eventually marry. What if she had and discovered Terry's problem afterward? She didn't have an answer to that question. Her parents had divorced, and she had promised herself she wouldn't.

Up ahead she saw the sign to Black Horse Pass. She turned off the highway onto the one-lane, washboard, dirt road. Slowing her speed drastically, she bounced along the stretch that led to her meeting place with Ronald Hoffman. Everything was in place. Part of the following week at school was for studying before finals—no classes. Exams didn't start until next Thursday. She should be back in time to give the tests to her classes. Perfect timing.

The sun sat on the horizon, a big yellow-orange ball. Streaks of red and purple threaded through the cloudless azure-blue sky. It was going to be hot today. She patted her canteen next to her on the seat. Granted she didn't know a whole lot about hiking in desertlike conditions, but she did know about the importance of water and had brought a lot of extra, besides what was in the canteen.

She pulled into a makeshift parking lot near a grouping

of piñon trees at the end of the road. Climbing from her five-year-old Honda, she stroked its hood.

"You got me here, although I doubt you appreciated me coming down that road."

She made a full circle, taking in the landscape. Behind her was the long dirt road. Ahead were towering mesas, the sun burning a path up their facade and turning the rock a yellow orange as though it was made of gold. Through the sheer cliffs wound a narrow trail, dotted with cacti, brush and juniper and piñon trees. Already the nippy bite of a desert night had evaporated, leaving behind the heat of a desert day.

Hearing a screech, she observed the flight of a bald eagle, hunting for its next meal. It caught an air current and soared, disappearing behind a bluff. She hadn't done something like this in years, but as a child she had enjoyed the family hikes—until her parents had gotten a divorce.

She wasn't alone. The Lord was with her.

You created this beauty, Lord. Awesome. Magnificent. Give me the strength and ability to make it to Desolation Canyon. I need to know that I'm capable of doing this. Please show me, Lord. In Jesus Christ's name. Amen.

Lounging against the back of her car, she folded her arms across her chest and waited, her gaze trained on the road. She checked her watch. Ten minutes after seven.

She wasn't too worried. There were some places where the road had practically washed away from some of the recent spring rains. Ronald had probably not planned for that.

But when Kit glanced at the time an hour later, she could no longer come up with an excuse why Ronald wasn't at the pass. And she had given him some of the money ahead of time. No matter how much she told herself not to trust people, here she'd gone and put her belief in this man. When was she going to learn?

She stomped to her passenger door and opened it. Grabbing the canteen, she took a swig of cool water to ease her dry throat. Her gaze caught sight of the manila envelope with pages of the detailed map in it. When she slid it out, she examined the area around Black Horse Pass. It didn't look too tough to negotiate.

After buying her equipment and coming out here, she could go a little ways and see what the trail was like. There shouldn't be any harm in doing that.

"Who knows? I might even be pretty good at hiking. I did okay once," she muttered and opened her back door to get her pack and walking stick.

She would go for an hour or so, then return to her car. She would find someone else to take her to the canyon, so she might as well start building up her stamina.

When she heaved the bag and slipped her arms through the straps, she swayed and began to have her doubts. She'd forgotten it must weigh nearly forty pounds with all the water she'd brought. Lifting weights might have been a good idea, and something she would consider when she got back. After refilling her canteen with water, she left all but one jug on the backseat so her backpack wouldn't be so heavy.

She found the trailhead and started along the narrow path that led through the pass into a broad expanse of canyons, cliffs and mesas. The sun intensified, beating down on her. Sweat broke out on her forehead after only fifteen minutes. She paused and took another drink of water.

An hour and a half later, enthralled with the vista, Kit collapsed on a medium-size boulder that had slid down the side of a cliff. She shucked off her backpack and dropped it to the ground next to the rock. She would head back to the car after she rested a while. Using the white sleeve of her shirt, she wiped the sweat from her face, then her neck.

When she reached for her bag to get a cloth to use, she froze. Slithering from the underside of the boulder was a rattlesnake, followed by several more.

THREE

*Kit hasn't come home. She was supposed to come back
here. She's out there without a guide. She can't go to Desolation Canyon without the best there is.*

The Guardian paced from one end of the room to the
other, kneading his hand along his nape. All kinds of horrible
scenarios flashed through his mind. Lost and wandering
around in circles. Collapsing from dehydration. Her body
broken on the rocks after a fall.

*Why hadn't she come back when Hoffman didn't show
up? How am I supposed to watch over her when she does
things like go off by herself? One day I need to teach her a
lesson.*

Frustration churned his stomach. *But not today.*

He'd gone to some trouble to take care of Hoffman, the
least she could do was cooperate and return to Albuquerque.
He didn't want her to go to the canyon without the best, and
he'd checked out Hoffman. He wasn't the best. His job as
her guardian was becoming harder and harder. At least the
tracking device on her car and the bug in her house helped
him keep up with all her activities.

She should appreciate the trouble he had to go to for her.

One day she would. He withdrew from his pocket his untraceable cell to put in motion yet another rescue, suppressing the anger building in him.

As Hawke pulled onto the road that led to his ranch, his cell rang. He slowed and flipped it open. "Lonechief."

"I'm so glad I got hold of you. Kit went to Desolation Canyon by herself this morning and hasn't returned home yet."

Zach's frantic tone infected Hawke with the seriousness of the situation. He glanced out of the windshield to the west, and his fear mushroomed. The sun had begun its descent. "Does the woman have a death wish?" His grip on his phone tightened until he was afraid he would snap it into halves.

"From what I understand she had arranged for a guide to meet her at Black Horse Pass. He didn't show up because he was in a wreck on his way there. There was a message on her machine at her office from one of Ronald Hoffman's associates."

"That doesn't mean she went in by herself."

"She never came by her office to hear the message, and she isn't at her house, either. I hate to say this, but she probably got frustrated enough that she attempted it on her own. She can't seem to find a reliable guide."

The censure in Zach's voice hit its mark. Hawke made a U-turn and headed toward the highway and Black Horse Pass. "I'm on my way to see. Hopefully she decided to go off and do something tame like researching in a book."

"Normally I would say that Kit is a very tame person, but for some reason she has become driven with proving herself right."

"Have you tried calling her cell?"

"For the past hour. No answer. Which doesn't surprise me if she decided to hike into the area on her own. From here I can't get there as fast as you can. Besides, you know that part of the country better than me."

Again Hawke peered toward the west. "I won't be there much before dusk myself."

"That's better than pitch-black."

"How'd you find out about this guide?"

"Her neighbor is beside himself and he called me. The police came by to see Kit concerning the guide."

"The police! What's going on?" Somehow Hawke managed to keep his fear for Kit from his voice, but not his worry.

"They came by to see Kit because the guide's office told them he was supposed to meet her at Black Horse Pass."

"But why are the police involved?"

"Because Hoffman's car accident wasn't an accident. He was forced off the highway. He was found in a ravine off the road. Someone called the highway patrol and said he witnessed it early this morning."

"Did this someone leave a name?" Hawke gripped his cell, pain shooting down his arm.

"No. He doesn't want to get involved."

"Yeah, I've heard that before. Any description of the car that forced Hoffman off the highway?"

"A white truck. Nothing else."

"I'll call you when I know something."

"Thanks. She's been a big help to me this year. I don't want anything happening to her."

Neither do I. Hawke switched off his cell and pressed his foot on the accelerator. Time was against him.

An hour later, the sun halfway to the horizon, Hawke

scrambled from his Jeep, parked next to the only other car at the end of the road near Black Horse Pass. Kit's red Honda screamed to the world she had gone into the maze of canyons by herself. When he got his hands on her, she wouldn't be too happy, and before he was finished, she would understand how dangerous her little stunt was.

He grabbed a heavy-duty flashlight and a canteen with water from his vehicle and started along the trail through the pass. Fresh indentions in the dirt indicated someone had passed through not long before. Someone with small feet. At least she was wearing hiking boots. He'd envisioned her in tennis shoes trying to negotiate the uneven, often pebbly ground.

As he went farther along the path, the sun disappeared behind the tall mesas. He passed evidence of a new rock-slide in the shadow of a bluff. With his flashlight, he checked to make sure she wasn't pinned beneath a large stone.

With the ticking off of the minutes, his heart hammered a shade faster. Heat, captured in the sandy dirt, floated upward to encircle him. Sweat coated his face and chest, his tan shirt soaked.

Visions of Kit, hurt, possibly dead, haunted him with each step he took. Scenes from his past threatened to intrude, bringing with them the pain he usually kept suppressed. It had been four years ago that he had come this way. He had promised himself never again. And now, because of Kit Sinclair, he was breaking that promise. He thrust his memories away, determined to focus on his anger at her foolish actions.

When he rounded the base of a sheer cliff, he saw her, off to the right in the dying daylight—or at least he thought it was her—lying crumpled on a boulder, not moving. His anger fled, to be replaced with the terror of four years ago all over again. He stumbled, nearly going to his knees. He couldn't carry a second body out of here.

Although it was cooling, now that the sun was behind the mesa to the west, sweat broke out on his forehead as he rushed toward her. A couple of yards from the boulder a rattling sound sent out a warning. He went still, checking his surroundings as he carefully slipped his revolver from its holster.

A six-foot rattlesnake, coiled, lay a few feet to the left of the large stone. His gaze glued to the rattler, he moved in slow motion, lifting the gun to aim.

"Don't." Kit's husky voice pierced the air.

He glanced at her, then back at the reptile. "What do you mean, don't?"

"Don't kill it. It's only protecting its home, which I think is under the rock I'm sitting on."

"So what do you suggest I do?"

"I don't know. I was waiting for it to go away like the other ones."

"Others! Where did they go?" Hawke scanned the area quickly then fastened his gaze back on the rattler.

"Back under this rock."

"A nest?" Darkness crept closer. Soon he wouldn't be able to see well enough to shoot the snake.

"Maybe. The others were smaller."

With his breath held, he raised the gun, aimed and squeezed the trigger, all in one fluid movement, hitting the reptile, which was poised to strike.

"C'mon. Now, Kit. Move it. I've got you covered."

She struggled to stand on the boulder, then leaped to the ground a few feet from him. Red scored her cheeks. She tried to steady herself as she landed, but instead stumbled. He caught her, shoving her behind him.

Although dusk eroded the daylight, he inspected the ground around the huge rock for any signs of more rattlers. Relief sighed from his lips when he saw nothing.

"Let's get out of here." With one eye on the boulder, he turned toward her.

"My backpack is over there with my water." She gestured to the dirt not far from the massive stone she'd sat on.

"Too dangerous if more snakes are under that rock. We're leaving it."

"But my water! I haven't had anything to drink in hours."

He unhooked his canteen and thrust it into her hands. "Drink while you walk."

He didn't turn his back on the area until he was around the bend. Although the urge was strong, he would wait until they made it to their vehicles before giving her a piece of his mind.

Once they were ensconced beneath the towering cliffs on either side, night fully descended, and Hawke flicked on the flashlight.

"Walk behind me. Step where I step." His command charged the air with his controlled terseness.

Although Kit couldn't read his expression, she didn't have to see it to know anger marked his every feature. "I only sat down on the rock to rest before heading back to the car. I didn't know I was going to disturb a family of rattlesnakes. Believe me, if I had—"

"You may think this is the time to have a little chitchat, but I don't."

"But how did you know about me—"

"Kit, in case you haven't figured it out, walking around

out here during the day, let alone at night, isn't always the safest thing to do. We'll talk later. You wouldn't want me to tell you what I think at the moment." He took her hand and settled it on his shoulder, then set out again down the path.

Cold darkness closed in around Kit as she gripped Hawke and followed in his footsteps. His flashlight illuminated only the small space in front of him. Her imagination ran rampant with what might lie beyond the inky shroud surrounding them.

After her unfortunate encounter with the rattlers, she pictured them poised ready to strike at any second along the path. Her legs tingled, vying with the patches of burned skin she hadn't managed to shade from the sun. Funny how a few hours ago she had been hot. Now she was chilled.

Exhausted, dehydrated, her head pounding against her skull, she put one foot in front of the other. If she had known what was going to happen, of course, she would never have hiked away from her car. At least while sitting on that rock waiting for the snakes to slither away, she'd had time to think about this whole situation. She had to convince Hawke Lonechief to help her…somehow.

Then suddenly, in the midst of her fear and weariness, a thought took hold. She had to turn this over to the Lord. He would make it possible if it was meant to be. One of the hardest things she'd had to learn—was still learning—was to give control over to Him.

A movement to the left made Kit gasp and jump to the right. "What's that?"

"Any number of animals." Concealed in shadows, Hawke came to a stop and swung around toward her. "Probably a rabbit."

"A rabbit I can handle." She relaxed her rigid stance.

"Running from a predator."

"Predator!" she squeaked.

"You sound worried now."

Although she knew he couldn't see her expression, she scrunched her mouth into a tight line of displeasure. "And you sound smug."

"I guess some good came from this. Now you know what can happen if you go off by yourself."

She had to convince him she was still serious about going to Desolation Canyon—with or without a guide. Otherwise she didn't have a chance of convincing him to help her. The only good thing she saw from today's incident was that Hawke had come after her. That gave her hope.

"Yes, you're right." She nearly choked on those words as she stepped closer to him. "I had a little dress rehearsal of what could happen if I'm not better prepared. I have learned a valuable lesson. Next time I'll be better prepared."

"Next time!" He snorted and spun around forward, shining the light down the path.

In the glow she saw him shake his head. "You didn't think I was going to give up my plan, now, did you?" She infused just a touch of mockery into her question. "You obviously don't know much about me."

When she settled her hand on his shoulder as he continued toward the road, his muscles beneath her fingers bunched up. He didn't say a word for a good ten minutes. She didn't like the idea of being this close to him, either, but one bad move in a day was her limit.

He halted abruptly, pivoted toward her and pointed the flashlight at the small space between them. An eerie radiance cloaked his harsh features. Anger vibrated off him.

"Make me understand why this trip is so important to you that you're willing to risk your life for some myth."

His clipped statement rivaled the nip in the air. Shivering, she hugged her arms to her chest. "It's getting cold and this isn't the place to have that conversation. Remember?" She could still imagine that rattlesnake's mate stalking her escape.

"Fine. Let's go. We're almost to your car, then we can have that conversation."

Not out here, if she had anything to say about it. She trudged behind him. Although the clouds raced across the face of the moon, for a brief few moments its rays bathed the end of the road, revealing his Jeep parked behind her car.

A sigh escaped her. She'd made it back safely. She'd had her doubts a couple of hours ago when a crispness set in as the sun began its descent in the sky. Trapped, thirsty, with water within arm's reach but unattainable, she'd curled up on the flat part of the boulder to retain what heat she had while she'd prayed for the rattlers to get tired and leave.

Heat. She needed heat. At the beginning of Black Horse Pass she hurried forward, relieved that her keys were in her pocket, not her backpack. After digging them out, she unlocked her door and dived inside, trembling as she tried to start her car.

Nothing.

How could this be happening? With her teeth chattering, she tried again.

"What's wrong?" Hawke appeared in her open door, bending down to look inside.

"I don't know. It won't start."

"Here. Let me try."

Kit clambered from the driver's seat, and Hawke climbed in behind the steering wheel. He turned the key, then glanced down at the lighted dashboard.

"I don't know why I'm surprised. You don't have any gas."

"Sure I do. That can't be it." She stretched in front of him to stare at the empty gas gauge in shock. "I filled up a few days ago and haven't driven much. I don't understand." He was too close; she quickly jerked back.

Removing the keys, he handed them to her, then pushed to his feet and slammed the door. "Well, there isn't much we can do tonight. I'll drive you back. You can see about your car tomorrow. It certainly isn't going anywhere."

Still stunned, she stood by her Honda, watching him stride toward his Jeep. He settled himself behind his steering wheel, the interior light shining down on him. His vehicle beckoned with warmth and a way home.

She proceeded forward, paused and glanced back. *I should have had at least a third of a tank of gas.* Yes, she had been focused on going into the canyon, so maybe she hadn't had as much as she thought. Had she been so preoccupied that— She shook that thought from her head and continued toward Hawke's Jeep.

"I'm glad you decided to join me." Hawke started his engine, then switched on his heater. "Since it's late, it would be easier if you stayed at my ranch tonight. First thing tomorrow morning I can bring you out here with a can of gas. If that's all you need, you can be on your way home. If it's more, we'll find that out."

"That sounds fine." Kit remembered some of the stories Zach had told her about the time he and Maggie had stayed at Hawke's ranch while deciphering the journal and map. This would give her more time to persuade Hawke to help her. "Why did you say if that's all you need? Do you think it's something else?"

Hawke pulled out onto the dirt road. "You didn't smell the gas?"

"No. I didn't notice anything."

"It wasn't strong, but I definitely smelled it."

"Which means?"

"Something else might be going on other than you not filling up."

His ominous tone momentarily wiped the fatigue from her mind as she sat up straight and stared at his strong profile, cast in shadows by the dashboard glow. "What happened to Ronald Hoffman? How did you know I was at Black Horse Pass?"

"Ronald was in an accident on the way to meet you."

"Is he okay?"

"No. I called the police. He might not make it. Someone forced him off the road."

"Forced him?"

"A white truck was involved. Do you know anyone with a white truck?"

"No. Why?"

"He was coming to meet you when the incident happened. That's suspicious, since you're looking for the Lost City of Gold."

"But no one knew I was. This time I didn't tell a soul." She didn't count Marcus because he'd found out too late and besides, he would never do something like that. He barely listened to her when she discussed her theory. Eating healthy and exercising were his passions, not history and certainly nothing to do with nature.

"It may be nothing. Road rage is alive and well."

Although his voice and demeanor were casual, Kit wasn't convinced Hawke thought it was nothing but road rage. But what else could it be? Their meeting had been a secret.

* * *

The Guardian adjusted the night-vision binoculars to follow the Jeep's progress as it negotiated the bumpy road. When it disappeared around the bend, he brought them down.

Good. Everything was working out just as he'd planned. It hadn't taken him long to puncture her gas tank with a sharp rock, and obviously they had been gone long enough that it was drained empty, since the car hadn't started. Now he was counting on Kit talking Hawke Lonechief into being her guide. Only the best for her. Anything less was unacceptable, because he took his job as her protector seriously.

FOUR

"I'm not going to help her. I'm not." Hawke's voice hard and determined contrasted with his calm, even strokes as he brushed his favorite mare.

But a picture of Kit curled up on the boulder flickered through his mind, taunting his resolve. Why did he feel like he should? Up until a couple of weeks ago, he hadn't even known she existed. Then Zach had asked a favor of him—to listen to Kit and help her if he could.

I can't!

Yes, you can, an inner voice countered immediately. *Let it go. Move on. It's been four years since Pamela died.*

He squeezed his eyes closed, drawing in one deep breath after another, the smells of the barn accosting him. The image of his wife's face, the sheer terror on it as she lost her grip—

No!

His whole body shaking, he erased the vision from his mind.

"Son?"

His mother's voice seemed far away, but when he blinked his eyes open, she stood only a few feet from him, worry in her expression. He looked down at the brush he'd dropped in the hay, then back up at her.

"Are you all right?"

"John Lighthorse has been doing a good job. I'm glad I hired him to help Roger." He stooped and snatched up the tool to continue brushing Justice.

"They've both been a big help to me."

"Is Kit taken care of?" he asked, unable to stay inside and listen to her discuss the canyon with his mother.

"When I left the house, she was getting ready for bed. She wouldn't admit it, but she was exhausted and I'm sure she was glad when I showed her to her bedroom."

"Yes, I imagine she was." Kit, defiant, standing in front of him with a determination he rarely saw, popped into his mind and disturbed his own resolve. *Her* scent, with the faintest hint of lavender, invaded his thoughts and blotted out all other smells.

"I gave her some salve for her sunburn. She'll feel it tomorrow."

Cheeks red, Kit had practically fallen into his arms when she'd leaped off the boulder. Although fear had leaked into her gaze, she'd tried to appear brave, as though encountering a nest of rattlers was an everyday occurrence. "It was a good thing most of her was protected from the sun."

"Except part of her arms and face."

"You would think today would give her pause in her pursuit."

"But it hasn't."

He twisted around and faced his mother. "What did she say to you?"

"That she intends to find a guide and go to Desolation Canyon. She isn't the type of person to give up on a dream."

"There isn't anyone who…" He turned back and stroked the mare.

"...who is as capable as you are to guide her?"

"Right."

"Then don't you think before she ends up hurt you should help her?"

Justice's reddish-brown coat reminded Hawke of the rocks that formed Desolation Canyon. He thought of the narrow pass she would have to traverse that could be bone-dry one minute and suddenly become a raging torrent from rains miles away. That was only one of the dangers she would face if she persisted in going through with her plan.

"This is your opportunity to put Pamela to rest. Think about that, son. Good night."

His mother's quiet footsteps moved away from him. He dropped his head against Justice's side. Guilt wouldn't allow him to let Pamela go.

I would have to go to the one place I never want to see again. But what if something happens to Kit that I could prevent? If I help Kit, would that make up for Pamela's dying because I let her down?

The next morning Kit grazed her fingertips across her cheek and winced. Her face burned. If only she hadn't taken off her hat and put it by her backpack, she wouldn't be feeling and looking like one of the mesas when the sun hit it.

As she headed for the bedroom door at Hawke's house, she caught sight of herself in the mirror over the dresser. Good thing she wasn't trying to impress anyone. Clearly pinkish red wasn't her best color.

Out in the hall she got a whiff of coffee brewing and the scent of bacon frying. It drew her toward the kitchen. When she entered, she found Evelyn at the stove removing the meat from the skillet.

"Ah, I wondered when you would be up." The older woman with her hair braided down her back and wearing a red, short-sleeved dress smiled at Kit. "I have to leave in half an hour for church, and I'd hoped to see you before I left."

"You should have wakened me."

"You needed your sleep."

Kit scanned the room. "Where's Hawke?"

"He went to the police station, but he'll be back soon. He told me he was taking you to get your car this morning."

"Can I help you with anything?" Glancing at her watch, Kit noted the late hour. She rarely slept past seven, and it was nine already.

"No, I'm almost finished. I'm making scrambled eggs. Help yourself to some coffee."

"Thanks." Kit padded to the stove and poured herself some, then took a seat at the table before a place setting.

"Did you sleep all right?"

"Yes. Great. I must have really been tired. I rarely get more than five or six hours." *Usually because I wake up from my nightmare and can't go back to sleep.* But she wouldn't go into that with anyone.

With a glance out the window over the sink, Evelyn took the frying pan from the burner and approached Kit. "Hawke's back. Tell me when."

Kit motioned for the older woman to stop after several spoonfuls of the egg dish. "Good. I hate to impose."

"I love having company. It can get lonely out here."

"Why don't you move into town?"

"This is my heritage. Hawke's. The ranch has been in my family for over a hundred years. I can't imagine living anywhere else."

As Evelyn put the plate of bacon on the table and sat,

Hawke opened the back door and entered. His gaze locked with Kit's, seizing her breath for a long moment before she looked away and concentrated on blessing her food.

"I see I timed it perfectly. I'm starved." He sauntered into the middle of the small kitchen.

"I left some for you on the stove," his mother said.

"I'll take you to go get your car after we eat. I brought some gas back to put in your tank." After Hawke dished up his breakfast, he settled into the chair next to Kit.

"Thanks. I'm anxious to get home and check on Mr. Hoffman. I hope he's okay."

"I called the hospital where he was taken. He is in a coma."

Kit dropped her fork, and it clanged against the plate. "He is? I—"

"That's awful. Where did the wreck occur?" Evelyn patted Kit's hand.

"On Interstate 40. From what I understand from the highway patrol, they are pursuing it as a hit-and-run. They're looking for the white truck, but the chances are slim they'll discover who ran Hoffman's car off the highway or why." Hawke dug into his scrambled eggs.

Shock still gripped Kit. "He may never regain consciousness."

"He might not." Hawke took a long swallow of his coffee.

"You think this may be connected to me?" Kit hugged her arms to her.

"Until the driver is found, we'll never know for sure why Hoffman was forced off the road. I did talk to one of his associates and the man was an aggressive driver."

"Then it could have been road rage. He might have cut someone off and made them angry."

Hawke nodded.

"What are you going to do about finding a guide, Kit?" Evelyn took a drink of her coffee.

Still stunned from the news, Kit lifted her shoulders in a shrug. "Start over, I guess."

"I'll do it on one condition." Hawke reached for a couple of pieces of bacon.

"What?" Kit's fingers curled around the napkin in her lap, not sure she had heard him correctly.

"I'll take you to Desolation Canyon if you get physically prepared."

"You mean go to a gym? Work out?"

"Not exactly. Give me at least a week to get you into better shape. I would prefer longer, but I can't be gone too long from my job. I have some vacation time coming to me. I want you here at the ranch. You have to agree to do what I say."

She could get herself into shape without him watching over her every move. She opened her mouth to protest his high-handedness and suddenly realized she needed him a lot more than he needed her. She had to agree if she wanted him to guide her into Desolation Canyon.

"Fine," Kit muttered, not liking the conditions of their agreement already.

"Good. We'll get your car, then you can go get your things at your house, because we'll start on your training this afternoon."

The gleam in his eyes unnerved her. *What have I accepted?*

"I'll fill your tank, then we can be on our way." Hawke pulled up to her red Honda, sitting undisturbed near the trailhead into Black Horse Pass.

After he hopped out of his Jeep, Kit clambered down and looked around at the deserted terrain. A lone hawk flew above her in lazy circles in the clear blue sky. Suddenly the bird swooped down and plucked its prey from the ground. She turned away, not wanting to see what happened next.

"This will get you to the highway and a filling station." Hawke recapped her gas tank and stowed the gallon jug in the back of his vehicle. "When we get to the main road, I'll follow you to the station to make sure you have enough to make it there."

Kit slipped in behind her steering wheel and started her engine. She released a sigh of relief when her car purred to life. The sound, though, confirmed she had let herself run out of gas. All she could do was chalk it up to being too preoccupied with her work to pay attention to the little details like a full tank of gas. But still, that wasn't like her at all.

She trailed behind Hawke's Jeep as he headed toward the paved road that led to the highway. As her vehicle bumped over the ruts in the dirt, her tired body jarred with each jolt. Only a hundred yards from the asphalt pavement, her car died. She pounded her palm against the steering wheel.

Hawke stopped ahead of her and climbed from his vehicle. His long strides chewed up the short distance between them while she tried turning over the engine. Nothing. Like last night. She shoved her door open and stood.

"That should have been enough gas." His eyebrows wrinkled together.

Kneeling on the hard dirt, he examined her undercarriage. When he rolled to his feet, he stared at the road behind her Honda. His frown slashed deeper.

"What's wrong?" The faint odor of gasoline hung in the

air, which immediately alerted Kit that she might not have forgotten to fill up.

"You've been leaving a trail of gas. You've got a hole in your tank."

"How?" Kit stooped and inspected the area under her vehicle. A stronger scent of gas assailed her nostrils. A small pool of liquid collected on the dirt beneath her Honda.

"I don't understand how this would happen. My car isn't that old." When she stood, she dusted off her jeans.

"I'm not sure, but I have a friend who can tow your Honda into town and take a look at it. We'll have to leave it here. I'll try to push it over to the side, so a car can get around it."

While she steered, Hawke rolled her vehicle a few feet to the shoulder of the road. After that, she joined him in his Jeep, and they finished the short distance to the paved highway that led to Interstate 40.

"I'll take you home to get some clothes and whatever else you need. When we get back to San Angelo, Bud might know what happened for sure." He completed a call to his friend with the tow truck, then headed toward Albuquerque.

"I guess one good thing came out of this. I'm not losing my mind. I did gas up after all."

"I'm glad you're happy about something."

She examined the hard planes of his face, his jaw set in a firm line. "And you aren't?"

"I'm not gonna kid you." He slanted a look toward her as he pulled out on the interstate highway. "I'm not happy that I'm escorting you to a canyon I think you have no business exploring."

"Then why—" She snapped her mouth closed. This was one time she didn't need to appease her curiosity.

"I'm doing it because if you went in and anything

happened to you I would blame myself for not helping you. You've made it clear you're going, one way or another. At least if I'm with you, I can protect you."

"But you're doing it under protest?"

"Definitely." He gave her a crooked grin. "This won't be the first time I've done something under protest."

"I get the impression you don't do much unless you want to."

"A misconception. We all have obligations that have to be met whether we want to or not."

Beneath his words an undercurrent of tension caused her to pause and study him. His strong profile gave her a sense of security. He was the right person to escort her. He would protect her from any natural threat, but who was going to protect her against him? There was something about him that enticed her to forget that her career was her life now, that she didn't want any kind of relationship with a man other than friendship.

Fifty minutes later Hawke drove into her driveway and parked his Jeep. "Who's that on the porch?"

"The mailman."

"It's Sunday. Why is he delivering something on Sunday?"

"Spoken like a cop, suspicious about everything." Kit threw him a frown. "His sister lives across the street, and he visits her and her children a lot. He's a wonderful uncle. When her husband died, he helped her buy her home."

"I get the picture. He's a great guy."

"We've become friends," she couldn't resist adding. "We go to the same church. When I'm not here, Sean keeps any package for me and delivers it later after work or the next morning. I had one stolen off my porch a few years back."

When she left the Jeep and headed across her lawn toward the middle-aged man with white-blond hair, Sean spun toward her. "I was about to decide you weren't home. I was going to leave you a note."

"Is that the book I've been expecting?" She hurried up the steps and took the package he held out for her.

"It feels like one. I came by last night, and when you weren't here, I decided to try again this morning after church. I missed you at the service. The sermon was especially good today." Dressed in a short-sleeved white shirt, a red striped tie and black slacks, Sean smiled, displaying a row of straight, newly capped teeth that he'd told her he would be paying for years to come.

"My car ran out of gas and—" she glanced toward Hawke striding toward them "—it's a long story. Remind me to tell you about it one day."

When Hawke joined Kit, she introduced him. "This is Hawke Lonechief. Sean Sullivan."

The blond-headed man spied the Santa Maria Pueblo Tribal Police emblem on the side of the Jeep and asked, "You had trouble when you ran out of gas?"

"Oh, not much. Just a couple of six-foot rattlesnakes." Kit flipped her hand in the air before digging into her purse for her keys. "You're welcome to come in. I'm packing."

"Packing?" Sean's tanned forehead wrinkled.

"Hawke has agreed to be my guide to the canyon. I'm staying with him and his mother at their ranch until we're ready to make the trip, so I'll be gone for the next couple of weeks."

"Do you want me to hold all your mail?"

"Would you?"

Sean nodded. "I'll also look after the house as I've done before."

Kit touched his arm. "You're such a good friend. If anything comes up, you can reach me at Evelyn Lonechief's at the Santa Maria Pueblo." Opening the door, she was aware of Hawke behind her, silent, appraising Sean. "I can put on a pot of coffee if you want to stay."

"No, I'm sure you have a lot to do. I'll leave you two. I'll be praying you stay safe, Kit."

As she entered her house, Sean left the porch. Hawke followed her inside with one last look over his shoulder.

"How many people know about you looking for the Lost City of Gold?" he asked in a tight voice when she shut the front door.

"Probably half of Albuquerque," she said sarcastically while breezing past him toward the back of the house.

"Half! Are you sure you didn't announce it in the newspaper?"

She whirled around and blocked his entrance into the kitchen. "For your information, Sean thinks I'm going on a hiking trip to see parts of New Mexico I haven't seen. I haven't told him about my research. The only people who know anything about what I'm looking for is Samuel, a research librarian at the college, and Zach. My next-door neighbor thinks I'm looking for a Spanish mission, the one you found."

"I've met your neighbor, but who's this Samuel? Tell me about him."

"Are you going to be this demanding over the next several weeks?"

"This is only the beginning. I don't go into a situation without knowing as much of the facts as I can. What does Samuel know?"

"Only that I'm looking at various Indian ruins around

New Mexico with special interest in the northwest quadrant. I've never used the words *Lost City of Gold* with him, only Zach. What do you take me for?"

"Someone who is in over her head and won't admit it."

Kit turned her back on him, marched straight to the desk in the kitchen and tugged open the long drawer. Removing an address book, she walked into the dining room and flipped through the pages until she came to the name she needed. Then using her cell, she made a call. The drill of Hawke's sharp gaze burned a hole into her back as she waited for Wes to answer his phone.

"Hello."

"Wes, this is Kit. I've got a favor to ask. Can you give my finals this Thursday and Friday for me? Something came up unexpectedly, and I have to go out of town for a couple of weeks on a project I've been working on. Since part of the week is for studying, I just need someone to cover giving my exams."

"Sure. Anything I can help you with?"

"No, I've got everything under control. I'm tracking down information on the paper I'm writing. The receptionist was making copies of the exam for me. She'll have them."

"What do I do with the finals afterward?"

"Have her open my office and put them on my desk. Thanks. I owe you one."

"I'll remember that," Wes said with a chuckle before hanging up.

"A colleague at the college?"

The sound of Hawke's deep voice so close behind her produced a gasp from her as she swung around. "Don't sneak up on me like that."

The corner of his mouth tilted upward. "I wasn't sneaking. I was walking."

"Make more noise next time. You're too quiet when you walk."

"Sorry. A habit I developed when I was young."

"You must have been a joy to raise."

His grin grew. "The perfect son. Who is Wes?"

"Just because you're my guide to Desolation Canyon, that doesn't give you the right to know everything about me."

"Wes now knows you're going to be gone for a while, working on your paper. I think that gives me a right to ask you who Wes is."

"Why are you so suspicious?"

"That's my job to be suspicious. Remember I'm a cop."

"Did you give Zach and Maggie this much trouble last year when you helped them?"

"No, because I know Zach can take care of himself." He folded his arms over his chest, his gaze singeing her. "Who is Wes?"

Anger inundated her. She would prove Hawke Lonechief wrong. Moving back into the kitchen, she dropped her address book back into the drawer and slammed it shut. "He's a history professor at the college. I was his advisor. This is his first year teaching in the department. He's become quite popular with the students."

"He doesn't know what your paper is about?"

"He's been in my office. I'm sure he's seen some of the books I've been reading. He may have a general idea. Why all these questions about what people know?"

"Just a feeling. There are a lot of things that have happened to you lately." Hawke rubbed his nape, a shadow darkening his eyes.

"I ran out of gas. That has happened to me before."

"You have?"

"Yeah, once when I was in graduate school I was supposed to meet the guy I was dating for dinner. I was delayed. He didn't wait for me. In fact, he moved to the bar in the restaurant and started drinking, then decided to drive after that."

"What happened?"

"He was in an accident. He walked away unharmed. The couple in the other car wasn't so lucky. The man almost died." The thought of her first serious relationship and how wrong she had been only reconfirmed in her mind the need not to depend on anyone else for her happiness. "Terry knew how I felt about drinking and lied to me. He pretended he didn't drink alcohol. He said what I wanted to hear. I'm so glad I found out before we got any more serious." She wasn't about to tell Hawke that she had already become emotionally involved with the fellow graduate student and that his lie had cut deeply.

"I've seen what alcohol and driving can do to a person personally on my job. Not a good combination."

No, it wasn't. Her own experience as a child living with an alcoholic father was enough to convince her. But there was no way she would elaborate with Hawke. Over the next several weeks she would be giving him more control over her than she ever had with another human being since she was a child.

The sound of Hawke clearing his throat pulled her away from her memories of a time she didn't want to revisit. She blinked and focused on the man before her.

"I'd better pack my bag." She hesitated, for some reason unable to move from in front of Hawke. His look held her captive as though he had roped her to him.

"Yeah, I want us to start today." He took a step toward her.

Although he invaded her personal space, she held her ground, still trapped in the snare of his gaze. "I haven't been exercising a lot lately."

"That's about to change."

Another foot disappeared between them. Her pulse beat jumped.

"And while you aren't working out, I want you to explain about your research."

"I can do that." Her words came out in a breathless rush.

Strains of Mozart's *The Marriage of Figaro* blared through the sudden silence. Finally noticing just how close he was, Kit quickly backed away as Hawke stuffed his hand into his pant pocket and pulled out his ringing cell phone.

While talking, he turned away, walked to the sink and stared out the window. The muscles in his arm holding the phone bunched. "So you aren't sure how it happened?" A long pause, then Hawke finished with, "Fine. We'll pick it up tomorrow. Thanks, Bud."

"What's wrong?" Kit asked, tension rolling off Hawke although his voice had remained calm.

"Bud said the rock that hit your tank had to be big to make the hole it did." He snapped his cell closed and slipped it back into his pocket. "Did you feel or hear anything while driving to Black Horse Pass?"

"No, not that I remember…"

"I don't like this one bit. Have you considered someone might be trying to stop you from going into Desolation Canyon?"

FIVE

One of Kit's delicate eyebrows arched. "Besides you?"

Standing in her kitchen, Hawke laughed. "Yeah, besides me."

"No, not really. We've gone over this. I've made sure it isn't common knowledge." She tilted her head to the side. "Do you think we have a problem? That someone is after me?"

"Probably not, but it pays to be cautious. I don't want you to tell anyone else where you're going."

"Should I call Sean and ask him to keep quiet about what I'm doing?"

"It wouldn't hurt. Otherwise when you don't show up again at church, he might say something, and before long everyone will know."

"Fine, I'll pack and give him a call in the bedroom. I shouldn't be too long."

"I'll wait out on the porch for you."

As she headed toward the hallway, he escaped outside. Leaning into the wooden railing, he stared down at the flower bed.

He'd almost kissed her in the kitchen. For a few seconds the fire in her eyes had appealed to him and sparked something deep inside him—until he had banked it. He couldn't afford to become emotionally involved with anyone, especially someone like Kit who intrigued him.

Then why am I taking her to the canyon?

He shouldn't have given in to his need to protect. But deep down he'd known when he'd seen her curled up on the boulder with a rattlesnake nearby that he would guide her to Desolation Canyon—if she were alive. He just hadn't wanted to admit it to himself or her. Now he was trapped into doing something he knew was a big mistake.

"Hi. It's Hawke, isn't it?" Kit's neighbor stopped at the bottom of the porch steps, shielding his face from the glare of the sun as he looked up at Hawke.

"Yes. Marcus Perry?"

"I wasn't sure if she would be coming home or what after her guide was in that accident. Is she okay?"

Hawke nodded, studying the man standing on the sidewalk.

Marcus shifted from one foot to the other. "I look after the flowers out here." Marcus mounted the first two steps. "Actually I'm the one who planted these for her—" he gestured toward the bed below "—to give her house some color. She has a black thumb and can't keep anything alive for longer than a week."

Hawke's glance strayed from the yellow and red roses along the front of Kit's house to Marcus's multiple gardens next door. "You must spend a lot of time in your yard." That was the only place Hawke had ever seen him.

"I tinker around my yard occasionally, but I don't have the time I wish I had."

"What do you do?"

"I have property I manage, and I write self-help books."

"Anything I'd recognize?"

"Do you read self-help books?"

"No."

"Then I doubt it." Marcus smiled when the front door opened, and Kit emerged from her house. His gaze zoomed in on the piece of luggage she carried. "Going somewhere?"

"Away."

"Of course. When will you be back?"

Kit's gaze slanted toward Hawke. "I'm doing some research, so I'm not sure. I'll call you and let you know if I'm going to be gone longer than a week or so."

Marcus considered Hawke for a long moment, then looked at Kit. "You don't need to worry about anything here. I'll take care of your flowers out here and anything else as if it were mine."

"Thanks. You've got my cell number if you need me. If you can't reach me on it, I'm staying with Hawke's mother, Evelyn Lonechief, at Santa Maria Pueblo."

Hawke took her bag and started toward his Jeep. There was something about Marcus Perry that bothered him. He'd been to Kit's twice and both times he'd talked with her neighbor. Did he do more than watch her house when she was gone? The thought unnerved him. He might not be interested in her work, but the man could be interested in the lady. When they returned from Desolation Canyon, maybe he should snoop around and run a check on her neighbor.

Five minutes later after saying goodbye to Marcus, Kit settled into his Jeep. "I never worry when I'm gone. Marcus takes looking after my place seriously."

"He does?" Hawke backed out of her driveway and glanced toward the man being discussed.

Marcus stood on the sidewalk in front of Kit's house, observing them. Hawke lost sight of her neighbor when he turned the corner at the end of the block and headed toward Interstate 40.

"Your neighbor is…interesting."

"He and Sean have been a big help to me. Between those two, I feel quite safe. I'm grateful Marcus works from his home. He's the one who called the police when someone broke into my house. Thankfully nothing was taken because he scared the person away. The next day he was there to fix my busted door and put dead bolts on every entrance."

"Do you have an alarm system?"

"I do now. I got one right after that. The same company monitors Marcus's house. In fact, a lot of the people on the street. He knows the owner. Marcus has quite a bit of property around Albuquerque and that company always does his security."

Hawke gripped his steering wheel so tightly his arms hurt. He forced himself to relax. Since he hadn't slept more than an hour the night before, he was tired. The added stress only made him wearier. And he was positive he would need all his strength over the course of the next few weeks.

Several days later every muscle protested the walk from the barn to Hawke's house, but there was no way Kit would say a word to him. He was waiting for her to tell him that she wanted to give up, that there was no way she would be in any kind of condition to hike to the canyon in a few days.

"Now I realize why John didn't show up for work this morning." With an effort, she managed not to wince with each step although it was next to impossible not to limp just a little.

"I gave him the day off. Since we were going to do his jobs I saw no reason for him to come and watch us work. He hasn't had a day off in a while."

"And you got free labor here in the form of me." Kit tapped her chest and regretted the movement of lifting her arm to execute it.

"I was right there alongside you while you mucked the stalls and repaired the fences."

"You nailed while I carried the lumber to you. You took the wheelbarrow out of the stall after I shoveled the dirty hay into it. Not what I would call equal duties."

"Are you complaining?" He gave her a raised eyebrow as he stared down at her.

"Oh, never. I did it gladly."

His laughter infused the silence of dusk. "Sarcasm. From you? I'm surprised."

"Then you don't know me very well."

He paused, causing her to come to a stop. "True. I don't. Maybe we should remedy that since we'll be spending quality time together in a few days."

"Sarcasm. From you?" She started forward, eyeing the six steps up to the kitchen door. Normally that wouldn't be a problem unless a person had run to the top of a mesa then back down again.

"Actually in this case, I'm serious. We've been so busy the past five days that we haven't had much time to just talk."

"And you want to now, when I can barely put two sentences together."

"Oh, I think you're doing a pretty good job of keeping up with me."

This time she came to a halt, stunned. "A compliment from you?"

"Okay. I know I've been pushing you, but you're walking better today than yesterday."

"Only because I'm determined not to show you my pain."

His chuckles drifted to her as he mounted those six steps. She wondered if she would ascend without groaning. At the door he waited.

She put one foot on the first stair and surprisingly it didn't hurt as much as the day before. "Hey, this isn't as bad as I thought it would be. Maybe I'm getting into shape after all." The scent of beef and onion wafted to her. "I thought your mother was going to be gone for dinner tonight."

"She left us some food on the stove."

Kit took a deep breath. "It smells like spaghetti."

"Yeah." Hawke shut the door after she entered the kitchen and approached the stove. "I had a grandmother who was Italian and I loved her spaghetti."

"You're easy to please."

He swung around and pinned her with a probing look. "You think?"

In that moment she had to say no because scene after scene of the past five days flitted through her mind. He had pushed her to her limit and beyond. Nothing she had done had pleased him. She ran too slowly. She didn't lift enough weights although her arms quivered each time she hoisted them up.

Facing him, she fisted her hands on her hips. "Isn't there a way to work out that's fun?"

"You haven't been having a good time?" His wounded look mocked her.

"No."

"You aren't at a desert spa. This is a working ranch. What better way to get into shape than to work physically?"

"Everyone needs a day off every once in a while. Even me."

"Is that a complaint I hear from your lips?"

"An observation." His gaze locked on her mouth, and her heartbeat increased.

"Ah. Didn't you tell me you had to go to Albuquerque the day after tomorrow?"

She nodded.

"That can be your day off." He turned back to the stove.

"And yours?"

"I thought I would go with you."

"Why?" They had been together so much the past week that the idea sent panic through her. His quiet intensity intrigued her and attracted her. She needed some time away from him to shore up her defenses before they headed into the canyon. He could easily take over her life, and she couldn't allow that. Twice she had been hurt deeply. She wouldn't allow it a third time, and the only way to ensure that was to stay away from men like Hawke. He was highly intellectual, physically capable of protecting himself as well as anyone around him and compassionate toward people. She'd seen how he was with others and how much they respected him.

"Call it a gut feeling." He shrugged and opened the cabinet door next to him to remove two plates. "When I commit to something, I do it one hundred percent. I've already spent time invested in getting you prepared. I just want to make sure everything goes off without a hitch."

"A hitch? What in the world are you expecting to happen in Albuquerque?" After washing her hands at the sink, she took the plate of spaghetti he'd dished for her and sat at the table.

"Nothing, and I want to keep it that way." He settled into the chair next to her. "The last time you went off on your own you got stuck on a boulder guarded by a rattlesnake and you ran out of gas. Not a good record."

"I'll have you know, technically I didn't run out of gas. I had a hole in my tank." After a quick prayer of thanks, she gripped her fork as though she were going to stab something. "One of the places I'm going is church."

"Is that a warning?"

"Frankly, yes. I know you aren't involved in the church Evelyn goes to, but you were at one time."

"How do you know that?" His jaw clenched.

"From what the people said when I went with your mother on Wednesday night. What happened?"

He started eating as though he hadn't heard her question. Minutes passed with quiet dominating the space between them. Although he hadn't said for her to mind her own business, his actions clearly conveyed that.

Lord, am I supposed to help Hawke through something? Is that why we've been thrown together? If so, how am I supposed to help if I don't know what's going on inside him? He can delve into my life, but his is off-limits. Show me the way, Lord.

Halfway through the delicious meal, Kit decided to end the silence. "What do you have in store for me tomorrow in the way of training?"

"Something different." A thread of tension remained in his voice.

"What?"

He looked into her eyes, a gleam catching fire in his gaze. "A surprise."

"Have I told you I don't like surprises?"

"A lot of people don't."

"I'm sure *you* don't."

"No, but then I'm rarely surprised. I prepare myself for all contingencies. That's one of the reasons I'm going with you to Albuquerque."

"You think I'm in danger?" She shivered at the thought.

"It's one possibility I have to consider. You *are* searching for the Lost City of Gold."

"Yes, and gold makes some people go crazy with greed. You don't have to remind me."

"Good." He finished his water. "It's settled. I'm coming with you."

"You want me to ride Justice bareback! Why?" Surrounded by the scent of hay and horse, Kit stood in the entrance to the stall the next day as Hawke slipped the bridle on the mare.

"It's a great way to build up your leg muscles. The only way you'll stay on Justice is by using them."

"Now I realize why you wanted to know how well I could ride a horse. But I've never ridden bareback."

"That's okay. You're going to learn." He led Justice out of the stall into the center of the barn. "We're going to the top of the mesa and rappel down its face, then climb back up."

Her mouth dropped open. "I don't know how to rappel or climb a rock face."

"You're going to learn. We may have to in the canyon, and I want you to be prepared."

"One of those contingencies of yours?"

"Yes. I haven't been there in four years. Things could have changed. Rocks slide. Water erodes. I don't know what to expect. The mesa we'll practice on isn't too tall."

"Falling from forty feet instead of fifty won't make much difference to my body when it hits the rocks below."

His gaze riveted to hers. "I'll be there with you every step of the way. I won't let anything happen to you."

Locked in a visual tether with Hawke, she believed him in that moment. She nodded her agreement and approached Justice. Hawke gave her a leg up, then went to another stall to ready his horse. She kept trying to put her feet into imaginary stirrups as she positioned herself as comfortably as possible on the mare's bare back. Although she had ridden some in the past, this experience was odd. She went through deep breathing to calm her nerves. But when her mount took her first step forward, Kit clutched her mane as well as the reins.

"Ease up, Kit. You're gonna pull Justice's mane out."

She shot him a sharp look at the amusement in his voice.

"I know you have to use your leg muscles to grip the horse, but try to relax, too."

"That's easier said than done."

"I want you to enjoy this outing. I thought we could have lunch at the top of the mesa before we rappel down."

"How about after? I don't think I could eat anything before."

"You've got yourself a deal." After slinging two saddlebags with equipment over his horse's haunches, Hawke swung up onto his gelding. "We'll take it slow until you get the hang of it."

"Then what's going to happen?" The question came out in a squeak as she pictured herself galloping over the land, hugging the mare's neck, her legs flopping around, with her desperately trying to hang on for dear life.

He ignored her inquiry and set his gelding into motion.

She stared at Hawke's back for a long moment until he disappeared from the barn.

"Okay, Justice. It's you and me. Be nice to me, and I'll be nice to you." Taking a last look at how far away the ground was, she squeezed her thighs tighter and tapped the mare's sides with the heels of her hiking boots.

When she emerged from the barn, Hawke sat patiently on Honor, waiting for her. At the sight of her, he started forward slowly. Between them and the mesa lay a semiarid landscape, dotted with brush, small trees and cacti.

When she caught up to him and rode beside him, she released her death grip on Justice's mane and held only the reins. The feel of the mare beneath her was so different from what she had experienced before when she had ridden, but it wasn't an unpleasant sensation. On the contrary, as she relaxed more, she realized she could get used to riding this way. She and her mare moved more as one.

"Justice and Honor are unusual names for horses. I guess with you being a police officer I shouldn't be surprised, though, at those names."

"Actually I named Justice when she was born, while I was home from law school. Mama gave Honor his name."

While he fell into silence, she searched for another topic of conversation. If she took her mind off what was to come, she could keep herself calm and relaxed. "How about this weather? It's gorgeous."

He chuckled. "Do you always talk so much?"

"Yeah, when I get nervous."

"Why are you nervous?" Beneath his black cowboy hat, he slanted a look at her. "You're doing a nice job. You haven't fallen off once."

His compliment suffused her with warmth. She dropped

her head slightly so her hat brim could shield the blush she knew colored her cheeks.

"Look around. Enjoy nature, the quiet."

She followed his advice and scanned the terrain around them. Its stark beauty appealed to her. Flowers littered the ground, adding to its allure. Off to her side a jackrabbit scurried away. A bird soared above her in the cloudless, powder-blue sky.

Halfway to the mesa, Hawke increased his gelding's gait to a slow canter. Kit gritted her teeth, clenched her leg muscles more firmly about the mare and followed suit. A warm breeze caressed her face as she kept up with Hawke. When she permitted herself a moment to enjoy the feel of the mare's movement beneath her, she began to flow with the horse.

At the base of the red rock formation, Hawke slowed to a walk and guided Honor to a path that wound up the west side of the mesa at a thirty-degree slope. Kit leaned forward slightly and let Justice trail several feet behind the gelding.

At the top she dismounted, the stain of sweat marking the horse where Kit had sat. Muscles in her thighs and bottom protested any movement as she rounded to the front of Justice and stroked the bridge of her nose. "You and I make a good team," she whispered to the mare.

Then, with her legs quivering, Kit slowly rotated in a circle, taking in the scenery spread out before her for miles. "This is breathtaking. I could spend all my time up here."

"Mesa Rojo is my favorite place on the ranch."

"Do you get up here much?"

"No."

She pivoted toward him. "Why not?"

"Are you ready to rappel?" He took the saddlebags from his horse.

"You know, we're going to be spending a lot of time together. You aren't always going to be able to evade my questions."

"Why not?" He removed his cowboy hat, a grin tilting up the corners of his mouth.

"Because I'm persistent."

"So am I."

"Well, I guess we have something in common."

"Ready." He walked toward the cliff's rim, facing his house, off in the distance.

"What about the horses? Shouldn't we tie them up or something?"

"No, and quit stalling. I'm hungry. The quicker we do this, the quicker I can eat."

She waved her hand in the air. "Go ahead. Eat. Don't let me stop you."

"Kit Sinclair, are you afraid?" He threw the challenge at her feet.

"Oh, all right, let's get this over with." She heaved a sigh and stomped toward him.

When she reached the edge, she made the mistake of peering over it to glimpse the ground below. Although normally not afraid of heights, she noted the long way down. The path they would take plunged straight down at an eighty-degree angle. She gulped and stepped away while Hawke unpacked the climbing equipment.

An hour later, with her arms trembling, Kit hoisted herself up and over the mesa's ledge. Crawling away from the cliff's rim, she collapsed and stared up at the azure sky.

When she peered toward the edge, Hawke appeared, the only evidence of his exertion a few beads of sweat on his forehead, whereas perspiration drenched her shirt and face.

She turned away, trying to summon the energy to get up. Drained physically, she couldn't find the will to move.

Blocking the sun's rays, Hawke hovered over her and offered her the canteen. Wordlessly she heaved herself up on her elbows and drank deeply of the lukewarm water before she thrust it back into his hand.

"Thanks, I needed that." After removing her helmet, she shielded her eyes from the glare of the sun and looked up at him.

"The one thing you'll need more than anything else is water. Don't forget to take drinks often. Ready to eat?"

"What I'm really ready for are a nice soft bed and about nine or ten hours of sleep, but since there's nothing around here even remotely like a soft bed, I'll have to settle for food until we get back to your house."

Hawke rummaged in one of the bags and produced several paper sacks. One he tossed to her while he kept the other. "It's not much, but it'll hold you until we get home."

The word *home* conjured up an image of them sitting before a roaring fire in the comfort of a living room, sharing an intimate dinner for two with candles lit around them that gave the scene a surreal feel. Blinking, she rid her thoughts of the picture, shocked at where her exhausted mind took her.

With shaky hands, she ripped open the sack and unwrapped the foil about the peanut butter and honey sandwich. Her gaze flew to his. "I feel like a kid again."

"It doesn't spoil quickly in the heat." He quirked a grin that melted her insides.

Hurriedly looking away, she concentrated on eating her

sandwich and apple while downing half a canteen of water. "That was hard work." With a toss of her head, she gestured toward the ledge.

"Overall you did well."

"You don't have to sound so surprised. I'm a quick study."

"Good. You never know when that'll come in handy."

"This trip into the canyon is going to go off without any problems."

"Why do you say that?" Hawke crushed his paper goods into a ball and stuffed them into his saddlebag.

"Because I have you as my guide. You know what you're doing. You've been there many times before."

She tried to ignore the darkening of his expression when she mentioned he'd been there before, but it was impossible. His casual bearing transformed. His jaw hardened. A nerve in his cheek twitched. His back stiffened. She'd trodden into a forbidden topic, but she wasn't going to back down.

"I'm sorry that your wife died in Desolation Canyon, but keeping your feelings locked up only makes it worse. You don't have to tell me, but talk to someone about what's going on with you." After Gregory's murder if she hadn't had the Lord to lean on, she would have fallen apart.

"You don't know what you're talking about. You live in your ivory tower, oblivious to what real life is like." He shoved himself to his feet.

"You think you have me all figured out." Rising faster than she thought possible, she faced him toe-to-toe. "Well, you don't. I know exactly what you're going through. A close friend was murdered right before my eyes." Although she hadn't really told him anything about Gregory, the second she'd spoken, she wanted to take back every word.

She hadn't intended to share that part of her past with him, but sometimes he made her so angry.

She thrust her trash into his hand, then pivoted and tromped to her mare. She wouldn't say another word to him. She'd already once waded through the misery Gregory's death and betrayal had wreaked in her life. She wouldn't go there again.

When she stroked Justice's neck, she tried to decide how to mount a horse that was almost seventeen hands without someone giving her a leg up. She scanned the area for a rock formation she could use as a stool because there was no way she would ask Hawke Lonechief for assistance. Ten yards away she found what she needed and grabbed the reins.

Hawke clamped his hand on her shoulder and stopped her movement forward. He turned her toward him, sympathy in his eyes. "I'll help—"

She shrugged from his grip and marched herself and Justice over to the small boulder. Without looking at him, she mounted her mare, trying desperately to ignore as much as possible the pain caused from using her sore muscles. She started for the trail that led to the bottom, her goal to get back to the barn and quickly escape into the house.

The whole way back to his house she felt his gaze boring into her back. She refused to acknowledge him, or she might do something she would regret—like tell him about Gregory.

At the barn she quickly brushed and rubbed down Justice before putting the mare in her stall. Then while Hawke was still occupied with Honor, she strode toward the house and let herself inside. As she crossed the living room, Evelyn emerged from the hallway.

"You received a call about ten minutes ago from Sean

Sullivan." Hawke's mother gave her a piece of paper with her friend's number on it.

"Did he say why he wanted to talk to me?" He wouldn't call unless it was important.

"No, but he needs you to call him right back."

Aware that Hawke entered the room, Kit hurried to the phone sitting on the table, her hand reaching for the receiver quivering. "Sean, this is Kit. What's up?"

"I called the police a while ago. I think someone's in your house."

SIX

"Have the police arrived yet?" In his kitchen Kit's gaze riveted to Hawke, who advanced toward her.

"No, but hopefully they'll be here soon. What do you want me to do? I can get my nephew's baseball bat and—" Stress laced Sean's voice.

"No, nothing I have is more important than you. Please don't go over there until the police have arrived. Tell them I'll be there as soon as possible. Thanks, Sean. I'm leaving right now. It'll be about an hour."

Her whole body shook by the time she hung up the phone and faced Hawke. "Someone broke into my house."

"Let's go." He dug his keys out of his pocket.

"I can go by myself. The police are coming."

"No. I'm coming with you."

"Fine. Let me get my purse." She didn't have energy to disagree with him.

"I'll be out in the Jeep. I'll pull around to the front and follow you to your house. You won't need your car next week."

He stalked toward the door while Kit made her way to the bedroom and snatched up her bag. She nearly dropped it. Hugging her purse and arms to her, she took a moment to compose herself. Someone in her house? Why? Was it connected to her search for the Lost City of Gold? Were Hawke's suspicions dead-on?

Sean sat on Kit's front steps, his elbows on his knees with his chin in his palms, his mailbag next to him. When he saw her pull up, he stood and rushed toward the driveway. "The police left thirty minutes ago, since there wasn't any sign of forced entry. They said if you discover anything missing to call them."

"Why did you think someone was in her house?" Hawke leaped from his vehicle, parked behind hers and slammed the door shut.

"I know the alarm didn't sound, but I thought I saw—" Sean twisted around and stared at the picture window "—someone moving around in your living room when I was delivering the mail. With that break-in four blocks away a couple of weeks ago, I didn't want to take any chances. I thought some burglary gang was moving into this area."

"I didn't know there had been a robbery." She laid her hand on his arm.

"I know I probably over reacted, but you know my motto, better safe than sorry." Sean gave her a small smile.

"Thanks for calling the police. I appreciate your watching my home while I am gone. Even if there wasn't a break-in, just knowing you and Marcus are keeping an eye on the place makes me feel better. Let's go inside and see if anything is missing."

Kit hastened toward her porch, searching for her house keys as she went. Unlocking her door, she started to step inside when Hawke halted her.

"Let me go first and make sure no one is hiding."

She sidled to the left, turned off the alarm and waited with Sean behind her as Hawke checked out the living room.

"It's okay," Hawke shouted from the hallway that led to the bedrooms.

Sean peered around her into the foyer. "I hope I was wrong and it was only my imagination. All the police could do was go around the house and look in the windows since I don't have a key."

"Marcus has a key."

"He isn't home. I went to get him before I called the police."

"It doesn't look like anything was disturbed, Kit, but you should check everything out to be sure." Hawke stopped a few feet inside the living-room entrance.

"I'll be right back, Sean."

Kit hurried toward the hall and made a quick walk through each bedroom. In hers she pulled out drawers and opened her closet but found nothing missing—she hoped. She couldn't be sure. Had she brought her address book into her room? She'd been unnerved the day she'd packed to leave for the ranch. Hawke did that to her.

The whole time she checked things Hawke lounged against the door frame with his arms crossed, his intense gaze following her progress. When she finished her search, she rubbed her sweaty palms against her jeans.

"Nothing." She approached him. *I think.*

"Let's go through the rest of the house."

Back in the living room, Sean stood before the picture window, staring at her front lawn. He whirled around when he heard them. "Anything missing?"

She shook her head, then made a careful survey of that area before she went into the dining room then the kitchen and searched them. When she returned to Sean and Hawke, both assessing the other, she said, "I don't see anything gone."

"I must have been wrong." Sean plowed his fingers through his hair, messing up his always-neat style. "I'm so sorry I got you here on a false alarm."

"I'm thrilled it was a false alarm. If not, I'd be dealing with the police and my insurance company. This way I came to town a half day early."

"You were coming back tomorrow?"

"I need to grade my classes' final exams and post semester grades. I was going to come back to Albuquerque in the morning, so there was no harm done. In fact, it'll be nice sleeping in my own bed."

Hawke wandered into the kitchen while Kit escorted Sean to the front door. "Thanks again." She leaned forward and kissed him on the cheek.

His face red, her friend waved his hand. "It was nothing. Anytime."

When she meandered into the kitchen, still keeping an eye out for anything out of place, she found Hawke standing at the large window overlooking the backyard. She inhaled then exhaled several deep breaths, forcing herself to relax.

The urge to fill the silence between them caused her to say, "I'm so glad that turned out the way it did."

For half a minute he didn't reply, then slowly he rotated toward her. "Your mailman mentioned some recent break-ins near here. Does this area have problems?"

"No more than other parts of the city. As you can see, Sean is vigilant as he walks his route. He seems to know what's going on in this part of town. I wasn't even aware of the robbery near here. And Marcus is the best crime stopper this block can have. He knows what's going on and usually keeps an eye on any activity on the street."

"Marcus doesn't keep regular work hours?"

"No. He told me once that he's his own boss and sets his schedule according to his mood."

He lounged back against the windowsill, gripping the wooden ledge. "How long have you two been neighbors?"

"Years. Since I moved here in graduate school. This was my aunt's house, and when she died, she left it to me. Why all the questions about Marcus?"

"I guess that's the cop in me. I want to know about the people in your life. I'm not convinced something isn't going on."

"So it's okay for you to know about my past and my life, but not the other way around. I don't need a bodyguard."

He quirked an eyebrow but didn't say a word.

"And I don't have any need for a cop, either."

"Have you thought that maybe someone was in here but didn't take anything because what he was looking for wasn't here? All your papers pertaining to the Lost City of Gold are at my house."

She gasped and shook her head. "But the alarm was on."

"An alarm can be disabled. The cop in me says either Sean was lying about seeing someone or there was someone and he got away. Marcus is the only one who has a key. For my peace of mind I want you to get that key until this is all over with."

"But he's a friend. What am I going to say to him?"

"It's nonnegotiable if you want my help."

"There's another option. Sean may have just been mistaken about what he thought he saw."

"True." Hawke pushed himself away from the windowsill. "That could be a third possibility. Is he often mistaken?"

"Sean could have been mistaken."

"Humor me. Tell me about Marcus."

"Why? You've met him."

"He has a key."

"Why would he want to know where the Lost City of Gold is? He doesn't care about things like that. He's comfortably well off and money hasn't ever meant anything to him. He's a good friend. He's helped—" She couldn't tell him about Gregory and how she had cried on her neighbor's shoulder when she had first discovered after his murder that her fiancé had a girlfriend in another city.

"He's helped you with what?"

She pivoted away. "Nothing."

"What, Kit?"

"You don't discuss your wife's death. Like you, I prefer to keep my past in my past. I don't discuss mine."

"Fine." His mouth tightened. "We're a team. Let's agree our past is off-limits. While you showed Sean to the door, I called Zach and told him we would be staying with him and Maggie tonight."

"Why?"

"I don't want you staying here alone."

"I'm not going." She jutted out her chin and crossed her arms. "I'm perfectly safe here. We decided that there hadn't been anyone in here. You go on and stay with Zach. You can come pick me up tomorrow morning at nine for church."

"You need—" He took in her mutinous look and knew he wasn't going to convince her to come. Short of him throwing her over his shoulder and hauling her out of here, she would be sleeping in her own bed tonight. She could be the most stubborn woman! "Fine. I'll see you tomorrow at nine."

He stalked to the door and slammed it a little harder than he should as he left. He'd go eat dinner with Zach and Maggie, cool off some, then come back and camp out in front of her house.

Sleep evaded Kit. At six in the morning she threw back her covers and got out of bed. She'd hated getting the key from her friend. He'd looked hurt last night when she had gone over and asked for it.

And to make matters even worse, with every sound she'd heard during the night she'd tensed, holding her breath, waiting for an intruder to come into her room. She blamed it on Hawke. She'd never felt this way in her own house before, even after the break-in a few years back. She wouldn't let fear rule her life now.

After quickly donning jeans and a large red T-shirt, she headed into the kitchen and fixed some coffee. Taking her mug into the living room, she opened her drapes and peered out the large picture window. Surprise flittered through her. What was Hawke's Jeep doing out front, empty? Where was he? For a brief few seconds, she wondered if an intruder had appeared last night and Hawke was lying somewhere hurt. Quickly, though, that thought popped out of her head to be replaced with the notion that the man knew how to take care of himself.

Then where was he?

She walked to the front door, opened it to step outside and look around, and nearly fell over Hawke's prone body stretched out in a sleeping bag before her entrance. Their gazes clashed.

"You've been here all night?"

"Yep." He sat up and rolled his shoulders.

"Why didn't you let me know?"

"Mmm. That coffee smells good." After pushing to his feet, he folded the sleeping bag.

He wasn't going to answer her! He was the most exasperating man at times. "Here." She thrust the mug she held into his hand, then spun around and marched into the kitchen to prepare another one for herself.

Hawke followed, his presence commanding the suddenly small space around her. His casual stance near the table sent alarm bells off in her mind. There was nothing casual about the predatory gleam in his dark eyes that took in her less-than-appealing appearance.

She combed her fingers through her still-messy hair, which she hadn't brushed yet. She lifted her mug and took a sip of the hot brew, burning the roof of her mouth. How could she think straight when she felt assessed and cataloged?

"Why did you come back here last night?"

"Because you wouldn't listen to reason." He half sat, half leaned back against the table. "I'd never have slept at Zach's knowing you were alone, so I came back to be here in case something went wrong."

"How did you sleep?" she asked him, hoping he'd had as miserable a night as she had since he was the reason behind hers.

"Great! The best in a long time." He mocked her with a grin. "You?"

"Oh, wonderful." Sarcasm dripped off her words. She blew on her coffee before taking another sip. "Do you want something for breakfast?"

"How about I take you out to eat?"

"Okay. I'll go ahead and get ready for church so we can

go from there. That way we won't have to rush back here.'
That way I don't have to be here alone with you. The very
thought of him camping out on her porch twisted her
stomach muscles into a huge knot.

"Let's agree our past is off-limits." The Guardian clicked
off the recorder, having heard the conversation between
Hawke and Kit a number of times. The rest was unimpor-
tant.

However, the part that interested him played over and
over in his mind. Lonechief's wife had died, and he didn't
want to talk about it. Why? Had he had something to do with
it? Kit had a way of being attracted to the wrong man.
Thankfully she had him to protect her.

He'd check out Hawke and find out the truth behind his
wife's death. He couldn't risk Kit being with the man if he
was a killer, even if he was the best guide for her. He hated
resorting to violence, but he'd do anything to ensure her
safety. She was his responsibility, and he took that seriously.

When the worship service ended and the congregation
began filing out of the sanctuary, Kit rose, expecting Hawke,
who sat beside her, to do likewise. Instead, he remained
seated, his gaze glued to the cross above the altar.

"Hawke," she whispered.

He didn't utter a word or move.

Concern shook her. She sat again and cupped her hand
over his on the pew between them. Even that gesture didn't
garner a response.

"Hawke, are you all right?"

"It's been a while since I stepped foot in a church." His
eyelids drooped closed, and he drew in a gulp of air.

"Why?"

He slipped his hand from beneath hers and twisted around to face her, staring at the pew between them. "I'm not worthy." He raised his head. "I—" Hawke's eyes narrowed on something behind her.

Someone coughed. She peered over her shoulder and caught her friend standing a foot away, looking down at his shoes, red tingeing his cheeks.

"Sean! I didn't see you when we came in."

"I was late. I went to see my sister." Sean shuffled back a step, still not establishing eye contact with her. "I didn't mean to interrupt. I just wanted to say hello."

When she glimpsed Hawke, his expression wiped clean of any emotion, the moment of sharing vanished. She rose. "I'm glad you did. Are you staying for refreshments?"

"I have too much to do at home." Her friend squinted at Hawke, whose gaze sharpened on him. "It's nice to see you again, Mr. Lonechief." Then he swung his attention to her. "Kit, if you need me to do anything while you're gone, just let me know."

"I will. Thanks."

As Sean hurried away, she scanned the sanctuary and noticed most of the pews had emptied and Reverend Collins was greeting the last person in line to speak to him. Her friend flew by the man without stopping to talk. Most unusual. Sean was shy and a proper gentleman with impeccable manners.

"I think you scared Sean away with that scowl of yours."

"Sorry." Hawke unfolded his long length and began sidestepping to the aisle, away from her.

She hastened to keep up with him. He made a beeline for the double glass doors leading outside. Long strides dissolved the distance between him and his vehicle. Wrenching open his door, he hoisted himself into the Jeep and started the engine.

She thought of the day she had stopped him from leaving the parking lot at the café. Would she have to do it again?

When she settled into the passenger's seat, breathless, she said, "Where's the fire?"

"You have a lot to do today—" his piercing gaze cut to her "—and I would like to get back to the ranch before it gets dark. I have a few things to check on."

"I just need to go by my office on campus and grade those papers."

"While you're there, I'll be at the library."

"Any reason?"

"I want to do my own research on the Lost City of Gold."

"Anything at the college library I've seen. I've shown you my data."

"I know. But while you're grading finals, I thought I would keep myself busy examining the data you didn't show me." He pulled out of the parking space and headed toward the campus.

His white-knuckled grip on the steering wheel prompted her to ask, "Are you afraid I'll question you about what happened back at the church?"

"Let's just say the moment has passed." He stopped at a light, his regard never straying from the road ahead.

"And you regret saying anything?"

"A moment of weakness."

"I didn't think you had any of those."

His gaze briefly skimmed over her face, before he pressed on the accelerator and shot across the intersection. "We all have them. I just try to keep mine to a minimum."

"I can believe that."

Ten minutes later Hawke parked next to the history building. "If you get through before I do, I'll be in the New Mexico room. If not, I'll see you at your office."

"You've been to the library before?"

"Yes, when I was helping Zach. And as a kid, I often went with Red. He's the one who motivated my love of books."

"I can see why. He's a legend around the school. If you need to get into the history building, my code is 54830." When Kit hopped from the Jeep, she turned on the sidewalk and said, "Sometimes Samuel works on Sunday. He's been helping me with my research. Tell him you know me, and he'll assist you in getting any book you need."

"I'll do that."

She swung around and strode toward the building, feeling Hawke's gaze on her. After punching in her code, she entered the lobby and crossed the large open space. The clicking of her heels on the marble tiles echoed through the two-story area, the hollow sound emphasizing the deserted feel of the place. She hurried toward the elevator and rode to the second floor.

She scanned the long empty hallway that led to her office. The hair on her nape tingled. Hugging her purse to her chest, she quickened her step down the corridor.

She fit her key into her office lock and promptly turned it. Thrusting the door open, she froze at the figure in the shadows by her desk.

SEVEN

In the entrance to her office, Kit gasped, stepped back and started to pivot, her heart practically leaping from her chest.

"Kit! It's me." Dropping the book in his hand, Wes Stanford moved from the shadows, his model-perfect face contorted into a frown. The harsh lines eased into a lopsided grin. "I'm sorry. I didn't mean to scare you."

"What are you doing in here?" With her pulse still throbbing a maddening pace through her, she gripped the door frame to steady herself.

"Getting this." He pointed toward the book he'd let fall to the desk. "A while back you said I could borrow it if I needed it for my research."

"I did?" She dragged her fingers through her hair, trying to remember if she had. Her mind muddled from exhaustion and stress, she couldn't recall. But then, there would be no reason she wouldn't lend him a text. She'd always shared with him. Then why the doubts at this moment that he was lying to her?

There was only one answer to that question: Hawke Lonechief was making her paranoid about the people around her because of her quest for the Lost City of Gold.

"I'm sorry. I should have said something to you. It was

a couple of months ago. I didn't think I would need it, but I hit a snag and thought the information in it would help me." He took a few steps toward her. "I'd better go. Again my apologies for frightening you."

She straightened away from the jamb and blocked his escape. "How did you get in here?"

His gaze swung away from her, all color drained from his face. "I was in a bit of a hurry the other day when your students finished with their finals. I didn't bring them to your office right away. I called the receptionist yesterday at home, and she told me where her master key was kept."

"She what?"

He looked straight into her eyes, saying, "Please don't get Kelly in trouble." Then he averted his gaze to a spot slightly to the left of Kit. "At first she was going to come all the way up here and let me in, but I didn't want her to go to that kind of trouble because I forgot to do it on Friday. I kind of sweet-talked her into it."

"I doubt you had to do much sweet-talking. Kelly has a thing for you." She forced herself to relax the tense set of her muscles.

Wes blushed. "I hadn't noticed. I've been so wrapped up in this research. It's not going the way I thought it would."

"What are you doing your paper on? Maybe after I get back I can help you."

"No, you have your own to do." He approached her. "I don't want to bother you with my problems. It'll work out. I just need to come up with a fresh angle." Only a foot away, he paused. "I'll leave you alone to grade your finals."

Keeping her distance, she moved into her office while he skirted around her out into the hall. "Wes!"

He stopped.

"Haven't you forgotten something?"

His eyebrows crunched together.

She walked to her desk and lifted the heavy book titled *Portugal's Empire in the Western Hemisphere.*

"Oh, yes. Sorry." Again red flooded his cheeks, and he rushed back into the room, grabbed the text and fled out the door.

When she strode to the entrance and peered out into the corridor, it was empty. Strange. She hadn't known Wes was interested in Portugal. His area of expertise and what she thought he would write his article on was Colonial North America, and Portugal had had little to do with that area.

After closing her door, she opened her blinds, and sunlight spilled into the room. First she examined her desk, trying to recall how she had left it. Yes, she could be messy at times, but it appeared worse than usual. Lying on the shortest stack of books were the finals. Right next to that was a folder with some articles and research on Coronado. Hadn't she put that in her file cabinet the last time she was in here?

Sinking down onto her chair, she retraced her steps but couldn't remember. The notes in that folder wouldn't tell anyone much, so why did she feel as if someone had gone through her office?

Would Wes have done that? She'd known him for years, first as a student and now as a colleague, and had helped him get where he was in the history department. She couldn't see him betraying her like that and for what?

Scanning the rest of the room, she noted the pile of magazines on top of a bookcase, the crammed shelves with texts stacked in every possible place. She needed a new bookcase. She needed someone to clean this office. The disorder mirrored her life at the moment.

She shook her head. She was letting Hawke's suspicions make her doubt a friend and colleague. Up until now, she'd never had a reason to distrust Wes's motives. When this expedition was over with, she intended to get her life back, and one of the ways would be to put a lot of distance between her and Hawke.

Hawke glanced up from the book to find Samuel White staring at him. The man immediately peered down at the computer screen in front of him and began typing. When he had first come into the library, he'd used Kit's name with the research librarian in order to see White's reaction. Now he wasn't so sure he should have said anything. He felt assessed, cataloged and discarded as unworthy, almost as if the librarian had a secret crush on Kit and saw him as the competition.

Perusing the written page before him, Hawke smiled. If only the man knew, he had nothing to worry where Hawke and Kit were concerned. At the end of a long day there wasn't anything left for Hawke to give a woman. After he took Kit to Desolation Canyon, he would say goodbye and never see her again. He would get her in and out of the place safely, and then maybe the guilt eating him up inside would ease. He had failed to protect one woman in the canyon; he wouldn't fail Kit.

After today's sermon, he knew he had to do something more with his life than wallow in his grief and guilt. He just wasn't sure what to do.

The words on the page faded as he thought back to what the reverend had said that morning. "God's love gives us a way to redeem ourselves, no matter the sin. That way is through Jesus Christ."

Kit's minister might believe that, but he didn't see any way the Lord could forgive him his sin. And if he were truthful with himself, no amount of good deeds would make up for it, either.

He didn't have to turn around to see Kit enter the New Mexico room at the library. He felt her presence the moment she came through the doorway. He heard her footsteps sound against the wooden floor as she approached his table. The scent of lavender, a soothing balm amidst the turmoil raging inside him, surrounded him before she settled her hand on his arm and slipped into the chair beside him.

"Find anything of interest?"

He set the book on the table. "Nothing that would convince you not to go to Desolation Canyon." He shoved away the tome, not caring to read any more about Coronado's crusade through the Southwest and his dealings with the Indians in his way. "Did you get the tests graded?"

"Yes, and final grades in. I'm free to leave—" Kit rose "—after I speak to Samuel."

The research librarian grinned as Kit came toward him. Turning from the computer, he stood, leaning into the counter. "I assisted your…friend, there—" Samuel tossed his head in the direction of Hawke "—with what he requested, but frankly some of the books he wanted to see didn't fit with what you've been looking at."

Kit bent toward Samuel and lowered her voice. "Like what?"

Hawke neared the pair. "I asked for a book on Chaco Canyon and one on the Aztec and Mayan trade practices."

She whirled around, her hand to her chest. "You need to warn someone you're approaching."

"Sorry. A habit of mine."

"Is eavesdropping on someone's conversation another one?" Kit asked.

"When I'm the topic, yes. But frankly—" Hawke looked at Samuel "—if you don't want to be overheard, don't speak so loudly."

"I was whispering." Kit's mouth firmed into a frown.

"Loudly."

She peered back at the research librarian. "Thanks for assisting my…friend. Samuel, you've been a big help to me. I'll let you read the article before I send it in if you want."

"You will? I'd love to." Samuel beamed, thrusting his shoulders back and puffing his chest out.

Hawke bit back his chuckle, but it was so obvious how the man felt about Kit. Poor guy. He wasn't Kit's type. She would become bored with him in no time. He wasn't— Suddenly Hawke brought his thoughts to a grinding halt. Why was he thinking about the type of man for Kit? In a couple of weeks she would be only a memory.

"Ready?"

Kit's smoky voice reined in his overactive imagination. He blinked, not liking what had been rumbling around in his mind.

"We need to go. Ready?"

"Sure. I've been ready to go since I arrived." Hawke strode toward the exit. "I just didn't relish watching you grade tests."

"I wish you had been with me." Kit started down the flight of stairs.

"Why? What happened?" He halted halfway down.

"Wes Stanford was in my office and scared me."

"Who is he again?"

"Oh, just a friend and fellow professor."

"And he scared you? That doesn't sound like a friend."

"You scared me a moment ago." Her eyes gleamed with mischief.

"But I'm not a friend."

"What are you?" The light in her gaze dimmed, and her mouth curved downward.

"Your guide."

She finished descending the stairs. He stayed where he was for a few extra seconds. He'd hurt her. He'd seen it in her expression, in the way she carried herself out the main entrance, her chin up, her back stiff.

Hurrying after her, he stopped her by grabbing her right arm in front of the library on the sidewalk. "We've been spending so much time together because I'm going to escort you to Desolation Canyon. That's my role in your life. I'm only your guide."

"I understand. Beyond that we have nothing in common to base a friendship on. Ignore what I said to Samuel."

He started to correct her. They had more in common than she thought. They both loved coffee way too much. They both enjoyed the sunrise and were a bit messy. The written word was important to her as well as him. They each had a past tragedy they didn't care to talk about. But he wasn't about to point that out to her. Instead he asked, "Why was this Wes Stanford in your office without your knowledge?"

"Looking for a book he wanted to borrow. My blinds were pulled so it was dim. I couldn't tell it was Wes at first. I thought it was someone…" Her teeth dug into her lower lip.

"What? Someone after your information concerning the Lost City?"

She nodded. "See what you've done? You've got me paranoid and suspecting all my friends."

"All I'm doing is my job. You should be cautious."

"I told you that you aren't my bodyguard. You're only my guide, remember?"

"Yes, you've made that point crystal clear." He began walking toward his Jeep in the parking lot at the side of the library. "Do you usually keep your office unlocked?"

"It's always locked. Wes got the master key from Kelly and let himself in."

"And you don't think that's suspicious?"

"No, he explained why."

"I'm sure he did."

At his Jeep, Kit opened the passenger door, peering back at him. "What I am sure about is that no one is going to follow us into Desolation Canyon."

The Guardian's hands quivered as he shut down his computer. Hawke Lonechief, the man he had maneuvered to be Kit's guide, had murdered his wife and gotten away with it. And he was going to be alone with Kit in Desolation Canyon where he'd killed the woman he supposedly loved.

The Guardian sprang to his feet and paced. He had to do something to protect Kit.

The next day Kit stumbled across the rocky terrain near the canyon system that Desolation was a part of. Darkness closed in around her, the quarter moon and Hawke's and her flashlights the only illumination. She couldn't even feel her shoulders anymore from the heavy weight of her backpack.

She bit back the words, *I thought we would be at your uncle's by now,* although she had almost said them on several occasions in the past hour since night fell. She wouldn't give Hawke the satisfaction.

His declaration when he had parked at Black Horse Pass
still grated on her nerves. "You have no business going into
the canyon. You need at least another month or two of con-
ditioning. We can put a stop to this right now." Okay, she
wasn't in the superb shape he obviously wanted her to be
in, but she had been determined the whole day not to
complain or to hinder Hawke in any way.

"This last part is a bit tricky." Hawke's voice carried on
the cooling current of air that blew through the ravine.

Just the last part? She would have to say the whole journey
had been a bit tricky. On a scale of one to ten she rated the
hike so far as an eight point five. And according to Hawke,
this was the easier leg of the journey.

"I'd hoped to get here before dark. I can usually make
it…" He let the unspoken implication be whisked away by the
wind.

Hawke stopped, and Kit nearly ran into him. She peered
around her and shone her light on the wall of rock before
her.

"We're almost there."

"We are?" She slowly rotated in a circle and only
glimpsed more granite, except for a narrow passage twenty
yards away. "We go through there?"

"No, we go up."

"Up!" She craned her neck and stared toward the sky. The
glow from her flashlight barely penetrated the black curtain.

He chuckled. "Did I forget to mention Gus lives on the
side of a cliff?"

"Why?"

"No unexpected visitors."

"He takes the hermit part seriously."

"He doesn't have much tolerance for people."

"Then maybe we should skip his…place and bed down here." Kit scanned the darkness and shivered. She didn't relish camping in the ravine. "I don't want to surprise him."

"We won't be. He knows we're here."

"He does?"

"For one thing we haven't exactly come in silently." Hawke waved his flashlight. "And this is like a beacon in the night."

"Since I haven't sprouted wings in the past hour, how do we go up?" Kit pulled the thick backpack straps together.

"Follow me. Put your feet where I do. The stairs aren't wide."

Kit fitted her foot on the first step, mere inches. With her heavy backpack, her balance was thrown off. She slipped back to the floor of the ravine. "Aren't wide" was an understatement! She dug her teeth into her bottom lip and leaned forward to counterweight the forty pounds on her back.

"Leave your pack. I'll come down and get it later."

"No. I can do this." She wasn't sure if she was reassuring him or her. But she knew one thing: she would scale this cliff with her gear.

He angled his light down on her, shining where she needed to place her shoe as well as what to hold on to.

"Thanks," she said, then muttered under her breath, "I'm sure you can do this blindfolded."

"No, but this is enough light for me."

What did he have? Superhearing? She gritted her teeth and kept her mouth shut while her fingernails clutched the small handhold.

When Hawke disappeared over a ledge, a gruff voice, rivaling the howl of the wind, boomed, "You're a week early and this isn't a hotel."

Still, Kit clung precariously to the cliff. She was only a few feet from the rocky shelf where Hawke was, but she didn't know if she should continue.

Suddenly his head poked over the edge, and he extended his hand toward her. "Grab hold. I'll help you."

"Are you sure? Your uncle doesn't sound too happy we're here, or at least that I am."

"I'm sure," he said with amusement.

She clasped his arm, and before she could catch her breath, he pulled her up and over the side of the ledge. Scanning the dimly lit shelf, protected by a rocky overhang from the elements, she lumbered to her feet. Her survey came to a halt when her gaze lit upon Hawke's uncle, a wiry man, only a few inches taller than she. His long, shocking-white hair hung about his shoulders in a wild array as though the wind had whipped through it.

But what made her gulp was the fierce inspection she received. She almost stepped back. Thankfully she didn't, because when the ageless man released her gaze, she glanced behind her. A sheer drop into a black void greeted her. A hand clamped about her wrist, and she was yanked forward against a wall of muscles.

"Stay away from the edge."

Hawke's own intensity imbued each word. She shuddered when she remembered how his wife had died.

"You know, it gets cold when the sun goes down." His arms encircled her and nestled her against his warmth.

She didn't correct him about why she was shaking. His wife's death wasn't a subject of conversation. His love must have run deep for Pamela. All her life she had wanted a love like that, but it hadn't been in God's plan. She would have to console herself with a satisfying career and her friends.

Before she became too comfortable within the safety of his arms, she sidestepped away and faced his uncle's "cabin." Cradled against the back wall of stone sat a structure made of adobe and logs that reminded her of what the ancient ones had built into the cliff side, only newer. Awed by the similarities, she ambled forward, drawn by the soft glow of light coming from inside.

"This is beautiful," she whispered, running her fingers over the sun-dried clay bricks.

"My uncle built this twelve years ago when he'd had enough of civilization and wanted to go back to his roots. I was able to help him one summer while I was home from college." Hawke's quiet voice came from over her left shoulder, the only sound vying with the wind howling through the narrow canyon below. "This fits him better than living in San Angelo."

"He lived in town?"

"Yeah, in the house I use when I stay there."

"There's a storm brewing." His uncle pulled open his wooden door and strode into his abode.

"C'mon. We need to get inside." Hawke swept his arm out to indicate she go first.

The second she entered with Hawke right behind her, she came to a stop and surveyed the primitive but beautiful room before her. A large area expanded all the way back to the cliff face. The floor was smooth rock, covered occasionally with woven, multicolored rugs. Indian murals, conveying different scenes from the past, covered the adobe walls. One opening, a blanket concealing what lay beyond, led off to the right and another to the left. A fire lit the spacious main room. Other than that the only other illumination was an oil lantern sitting on a low table with stacks of large pillows around it. Besides that piece of furniture, there were two comfortable-looking chairs, made from tree limbs, by the fireplace.

"Sit." Hawke's uncle gestured toward the pillows, took the lantern off the table, then sauntered toward the opening on the left.

When he pushed the blanket to the side, Kit saw what looked like a crude kitchen. "He doesn't say much," she said as she turned back to Hawke.

"No, he never did. That's why this suits him. He's comfortable with himself."

Kit eased down onto the thick pillows, feeling as though she had stepped back into the past. As a historian, the thought excited her. "I don't think I could do this for very long. I need to be around people."

"You aren't content with where you are in your life?"

"I didn't say that. I enjoy my alone time, but I also like to be around others."

"There's something to be said about this kind of life with no trappings of the modern world to burden you."

She gestured at the room. "You could do this?"

"For about a week." Laughter wove through his voice, and the sides of his eyes crinkled in a smile.

"So you aren't content with where you are in your life?"

He pinned her with a sharp look, all evidence of humor gone from his expression. "I like my work."

"I didn't ask that."

Vulnerability crept into his dark eyes. His regard delved into her for a few seconds before he twisted away and squinted toward the left, pushing himself to his feet. "Here, let me help you."

"Sit, boy." His uncle shuffled toward the table with a crude wooden tray laden with food.

The feast he presented surprised Kit. How could he fix something like this so quickly? Cooked meat sat on a bed of rice on top of a plate that was a piece of flat bread. A clay pitcher was accompanied by a bowl of some kind of berries and another one with what appeared to be slices of steamed cacti.

After Gus took his seat and poured a light-brown liquid into cups and put them in front of her and Hawke, he asked, "Why are you here?"

After blessing her food, Kit lifted her gaze to Hawke's uncle. "I'm the reason we're here. Hawke's taking me into Desolation Canyon."

His uncle didn't say a word, but his attention zeroed in on his nephew.

"Kit is a history professor at the same college as Zach. She's looking for the Lost City of Gold." Hawke sipped his tea.

Kit gripped her fork, preparing herself for the older man's ridicule. Instead, a thoughtful expression carved deeper lines into his sun-darkened skin.

"I see." Again Gus's shrewd regard took her in. "Do you have an area in mind?"

His question drew her forward. Clasping the side of the table, she leaned into it. "Yes. I think it's connected to the mission Hawke found. The Spanish often built their missions on top of Indian structures."

"So you think it's under the old mission ruins?" Gus asked.

"Or somewhere near. The Indians would have selected the most strategic place in the canyon. The Spanish would be drawn to that, too."

"At the mission I found pottery shards and other evidence

of the Indians' presence about the site, but nothing to indicate a City of Gold." Gus drank from his cup.

"Hawke, you didn't tell me this. There are probably Indian ruins under the mission." Irritation strengthened her voice.

"Which, as you've said before, isn't unusual."

"None of that makes any difference." Gus turned to Hawke. "The spring rains two years ago changed the canyon. Flooded part of it. The old way to go in is gone."

Hawke straightened. "It's shut off completely now?"

"No, but the way is harder." Gus glanced toward her. "Rough, nearly impossible terrain."

"But not impossible?" Kit's fingernails dug into the wooden table.

"No, but it would be for you." Gus began eating his food.

Although Kit wanted to pursue the conversation, a look from Hawke warned her to be quiet. She concentrated on eating her meat dish, but the knot forming in her stomach limited her appetite. She hadn't come all this way to turn back now.

After the silent dinner, Kit escaped outside to gather her scattered thoughts. She heard Hawke talking to his uncle, their low murmurs communicating a heated discussion between them. Hugging her arms to her, she moved out from the safety of the overhang, welcoming the cool wind whipping past her. A scent of rain hung in the air.

Lord, You didn't bring me here only to have me go back. What do I do? I need Your help.

Lightning flashed in the dark sky to the south. Thunder rumbled around her, causing the stones beneath her to vibrate. Although cold, she couldn't bring herself to go back into the house.

She sat near the edge with her legs curled up against her chest. Her hair danced about her as she stared into the blackness beyond the cliff. A few droplets splashed on her, but still she didn't want to return to the house and learn that Hawke was taking her back tomorrow.

Another bright streak ionized the air, followed by a loud boom. She quaked and tightened her arms around her jeans-clad legs. The wind smelled of charred wood as if the lightning had struck a tree nearby.

Hawke folded his long length on the ground next to her, his gaze trained on a spot in the distant night. "It's going to rain soon. You need to come inside."

"I know." She didn't move nor did he.

The elements raged to the south of her, more strikes hitting the ground, more explosive sounds rolling down the canyon below her. Rain splattered the ledge at the far end.

When the sky brightened for a few seconds, she caught sight of the other side of the narrow, steep gorge. The rocky facade appeared afire for that brief moment in time. Then darkness blinked in around her again, giving her a feeling she and Hawke were the only two people in the world.

"My uncle doesn't want to show me the new way to get into the canyon."

The words she'd dreaded electrified the air as if the lightning had blasted the stone surface between them. "Can't we try the old way?"

"No."

The Guardian brought the night-vision-equipped binoculars to his eyes and stared up at Kit sitting on the cliff with *him*. Anger spoiled her beautiful features, reflecting the expression on *his* face.

He wished he knew what they were saying, but one thing was for sure. Kit wasn't happy with Lonechief.

It was a good thing he had followed them since this morning. He would get rid of the man before something awful happened to Kit.

Cold rain pelted him, but he didn't care. He wouldn't take his attention off her. When they slept, he would climb to the top of the mesa in front of them and position himself across from the overhang. His opportunity would come in the morning. Beneath his slicker, he patted his high-powered rifle, confident he wouldn't miss Lonechief.

EIGHT

The crack of the rifle drove all other sounds from Kit's mind. The sight of him collapsing before her drenched her in shocked helplessness. Stumbling forward…

Kit's eyes snapped open. Her chest heaved, darkness enveloping her. Panic permeated her. Her panting resonated through the complete silence.

Where am I?

Not the church.

Just the nightmare. Again.

When she forced herself up onto her elbows, trying to see into her inky surroundings, the softness beneath her prodded her memory.

I'm in Hawke's uncle's bedroom. They're in the main room.

Slowly the panic receded; the heart-pounding fear vanished. Easing back onto the stack of animal pelts that served as Gus's bed, Kit dragged deep, calming breaths into her lungs, orienting herself to the present.

Hawke had said he would talk to his uncle, see if he could convince him to take them at least as far as the entrance into Desolation Canyon. She prayed he was successful.

Someone cleared his throat on the other side of the blanket that covered the opening. "Kit?"

"Yes?" She sat up.

Hawke peered into the room, the light he held casting his features in a golden glow. "We're leaving. You need to get up, get dressed." He placed the lantern on the floor by the opening to the outer room.

"What time is it?"

"Four."

"In the morning! It'll be dark."

"I know, but Gus has agreed to take us to the canyon. He says we need to be there by noon and through the narrow gorge that leads us into it."

"Why the rush?" She swung her legs to the floor, trying not to picture descending the stairs to the overhang in the dark. One false move and— She quaked.

"Because of the increased chance of a thunderstorm occurring. We have to be through the gorge."

"Why?" She rose, dressed in her sweatshirt and jeans that she'd slept in.

"You don't want to be caught in a flash flood."

Another tremor slithered down her spine. She'd heard of the danger of a flash flood. "This gorge is a riverbed?"

"Not exactly. One of the only places the water can leave the canyon fast is through this narrow ravine, hence we don't want to be caught in it if it rains even miles away."

He left the lantern with her so she could get ready, which didn't take long as she'd worn her clothes to bed. When she entered the main room, Gus hefted his pack onto his back, then went out through the front door.

Her stomach rumbled. "No coffee, breakfast?"

"We'll eat on the move when it gets light." Hawke followed his uncle from the dwelling.

After digging out her flashlight, Kit hurried to do likewise. Stumbling on an uneven surface, she caught herself before going down onto her knees. She quickly looked at the two men and noticed that Gus had witnessed her mishap. Straightening her backpack, she set her features in a determined expression and ignored his penetrating gaze.

Gus went first down the side of the cliff without the use of a light to illuminate his way.

When he'd been gone a few minutes, Hawke approached her near the edge. "It's your turn. Use your flashlight. I'll be right behind you." He tied a rope around her, then fastened it to him. "This is only a precaution."

Relieved at the security line, Kit backed down the steps, gingerly feeling for the next one as she made her descent. Although a chill clung to the night, sweat poured off her, dripping into her eyes. Pausing, she blinked and rubbed her face along the top of her sweatshirt sleeve.

"Okay?"

Even though she couldn't see Hawke's expression, she heard the concern in his question. "Fine." Even if she hadn't been, she wouldn't have admitted it to him.

When her foot settled on the firm ground at the bottom of the ravine, she sighed and crumpled against the wall. She tried to untie the rope around her, but her hands trembled. Finally giving up, she waited for Hawke to sever their connection.

He slipped the link off himself first, then her. Coiling the rope, he stuffed it in his backpack. After Gus clicked on his flashlight, he started down the chasm at a fast clip. Hawke indicated she go next. She hurried to keep up, centering all her attention on the small patch of lit ground in front of her.

The sound of something bouncing off the wall of the narrow canyon caused her to stop. She stared in the direction of the noise as a medium-size rock landed a few feet from her.

"Keep moving," Hawke said.

"But that—" she shone her light on the stone with a diameter of about six inches "—almost hit us."

"Almost doesn't count. Gus is already halfway down the ravine."

In her book "almost" counted, but she wasn't going to argue with Hawke. She knew the dangers.

The rock he'd accidentally knocked off the top of the mesa hit the floor of the ravine below him, nearly striking Kit. The Guardian rose and wanted to let out a scream of frustration.

They left in the middle of the night!

Regretting his need for sleep, he smashed his fist into his palm, wishing it were Lonechief's face. Now he had to follow the trio. The murderer should be dead in a few hours when the sun came up.

Kit was causing him a lot of trouble, and he wasn't even sure at the moment if she appreciated it.

Out in the open with nothing to shade her, Kit pulled the hat down lower on her head to shield her as much as possible from the blazing sun. Trudging behind Gus, she twisted the cap off her canteen, then took a long swig.

Up ahead jagged peaks and mesas dominated the landscape, their height daunting. The sun rays set them afire, an orange-red radiance to the rocks.

"Is that our destination?" she asked, peering back at Hawke a few paces behind her.

"Yep."

She checked her watch. "It's eleven. We'll make it in time."

Hawke studied the cloudless sky around them. "I don't think we needed to worry, but it never hurts to be cautious."

She hated asking for a favor, but after walking nearly eight hours, she needed to rest. "This time can we sit while we eat our lunch?"

"Hungry?"

"As a matter of fact, yes. I think I was hungry right after our breakfast."

Laughter pealed from him. "We'll rest. I think we can afford to do that." He pointed toward the shade of the cliff. "We'll stop up there where it's cooler."

Cooler was good. She'd shed her sweatshirt not long after the sun had risen. Body lavished with sunscreen, she still made it a point to walk in any shaded area she encountered.

Twenty minutes later, as they approached a narrow gap in the cliff, Hawke said, "Gus, let's rest and eat lunch before heading into the canyon."

The old man started to say something, contemplated Kit for a few seconds and shrugged. "Half an hour. No more."

The moment the shadow of the mesa encompassed her, she collapsed onto a small boulder and dropped her chin against her chest. Her body ached in places she hadn't realized it could. Even when she had been working out preparing for this trek, she hadn't hurt this much. Her muscles objected in fatigue, but she wouldn't say a word to Hawke. He was only here because of her.

After a couple of minutes she tore into her backpack and withdrew her lunch, a peanut butter and honey sandwich, a power bar and water. Hawke sank down near her while Gus disappeared in the thin opening in the wall.

"My uncle's going to check things out."

"If we need to go, we can," she reluctantly said, finishing the last bite of her sandwich in a hurry.

"No, you rest for now. Gus isn't one to sit for long."

"Try not at all."

Hawke chuckled, then took a sip of his water. "Yeah, that kinda sounds like him. He wanted to look over the gorge first."

"He's amazing. How old is he?"

"Seventy-five."

Kit's mouth dropped open. The wiry little man had more energy than she did at thirty. "When I get back, I'm going to start exercising every day. I can't let a seventy-five-year-old man run rings around me. Don't tell my friends. It would be embarrassing."

"How do you think I feel? I've had to live it down all my life."

Kit stared into Hawke's sheepish expression and burst out laughing. "Somehow I don't think it's been a problem for you. I have a feeling you've been able to hold your own with him."

Gus returned and sat across from them. "There's evidence of a recent flood. Finish up. Let's go."

"What if we encounter a flash flood?" Kit stuffed the last bite of her power bar into her mouth.

"You won't be able to outrun it so try to get to high ground, if possible." Hawke capped his water canteen and stood, rolling his shoulders.

"I'm ready." Reluctantly Kit pushed to her feet, stretching to ease the tenseness in her muscles.

Again she fell into step behind Gus, with Hawke taking up the rear. When she entered the narrow cut in the stone face of the cliff, she immediately scanned the area for high ground. But sheer rocky surfaces shot up toward the thin patch of baby-blue sky she glimpsed overhead.

"This is a canyon?" Able to touch both sides of the ravine

at the same time if she stretched out her arms, she hurried her pace to keep up with Gus.

"Gus told me some seismic activity opened this up when he was a young man, and over the years the water has further eroded it into what we have now."

The thought of an earthquake occurring while surrounded by all this rock almost trumped her fear of a flash flood happening. Her steps quickened even more until she was only a few feet from Gus. A couple hundred yards up ahead the area widened, and she discovered some higher ground where some boulders had fallen. In a stubby tree growing out of a crack in the stone facade above her, a water-smoothed, dead branch hung on a limb as though it had been snatched up as a flood raced by.

This was probably not the time to tell Hawke she couldn't swim well, actually had a fear of water. A memory of almost drowning at Lake Powell as a child of eight flashed into her mind as quickly as a flood would through this opening in the rocks. Frigid in the midst of the heated day, she scrubbed her hands up and down her arms.

Hawke appeared on the right side of her a step back. "We're almost at the end."

She focused on rough terrain, shutting the door on yet another memory she never wanted to relive. "No wonder this place isn't on the ten most visited spots in New Mexico."

"If this is the site of the Lost City of Gold, then be glad it isn't."

"Yeah, you've got a point."

Gus disappeared around a bend. When Kit caught up with him, she came to a stop and gulped, barely coating her parched throat. At the exit, a massive rock slide covered the opening into the canyon.

"We'll have to go over. This looks recent." Hawke and his uncle inspected the boulders lying in their path.

"Yes. Within the last month." Gus climbed up on a stone. "But shouldn't be hard to go over."

When she looked up five or six stories to the top of the obstacle, she had her doubts about that.

"I'll go next and help you up. Think of this as a staircase." Hawke hopped up behind his uncle and turned toward her.

This was when she wished she were at least half a foot taller. Being petite definitely put her at a disadvantage.

Almost two hours later Kit sat against the cliff, enjoying its coolness, while Hawke investigated the rock slide they had clamored over and Gus went in search of a natural spring nearby to replenish their water. To her there was nothing fascinating in the pile of boulders, but she'd learned that Hawke had once thought of becoming a geologist.

Stretching out before her was Desolation Canyon with high walls on all sides, cutting it off from the world. She felt as if she were in the center of a large granite bowl, oblong shaped. In the distance several contrastive colors—vermillion to canary—strewed the landscape. Trees no taller than her sprang up from the semidesert floor, blanketed with various shades of seaweed green and earthy tan. There was something almost tranquil about the terrain in front of her. A different kind of beauty but nevertheless God's.

Hawke squatted to examine the ground at the base of the largest stone in the rock slide, near the base of the cliff. Digging in the dirt, he scooped it away from a rock and bent closer to inspect it further.

His movement mesmerized her. He had an efficiency about him that spoke of a man who wasted nothing. She could watch him for hours. She should look away before he caught her staring at him. Out of the corner of her eye Kit saw a large stone plunging toward him, dislodging more on its rapid descent.

"Hawke!" She vaulted to her feet, dashing forward.

In a split second, he glanced at her then above him as the sound of the rocks falling magnified tenfold. "Stop," he shouted as he flew to the side.

Kit went rigid, her gaze transfixed on the pelting stones hitting the earth, the largest one missing Hawke by mere inches. One of the smaller ones struck him on the back, sending him to the ground while another slammed into the soil near her. She tensed.

Only seconds later quiet reigned in the canyon while dust clogged the air. The screech of a hawk above propelled Kit into motion. Closing the short distance between them, she knelt in the dirt beside him; her body was racked with coughs while his still one frightened her.

"Hawke? Are you all right?" She reached out to touch the side of his neck.

He stirred, his back rising in a deep breath. She sagged against the ground, her heart beating so fast her blood pressure must have shot up forty points. Slowly he rolled over and pushed himself to a sitting position, all color drained from his dust-covered face, his own coughs echoing through the canyon.

He slumped forward, groaning. "I was engrossed in the petroglyph I found. I know better than that. Thanks for the warning."

"How hurt are you?" She peered at the large boulder a foot away then at their surroundings. Slowly the dust settled back to earth.

He rotated and twisted his torso. "It just knocked the breath from me. Nothing's broken, but I'm gonna be sore for days." He stood up, holding his hand out for her. "It could have been a lot worse."

Kit took hold of him and rose. The second she was on her feet her legs seemed to liquefy and a violent trembling roiled through her body. Hawke's arms encircled her and pressed her against his chest.

"I'm okay, Kit, thanks to you. One second later..."

She lifted her head to stare up into his face. His gaze ensnared hers, a momentary bond between them reaching across all their differences to connect her to him as she'd never felt. She wanted to melt against him, forget that they were in the middle of nowhere, miles from civilization.

She opened her mouth, but he laid his finger over her lips. Whatever she was going to say evaporated from her mind. All her senses converged on him, hair tousled, a thin layer of dirt tinting his skin a lighter shade. A glint in his dark eye captivated her.

He bent his head toward hers, his finger slipping across her cheek until he plowed his hand into her hair and held her still. She tingled where his warm touch grazed. When he settled his mouth on hers, she dissolved against him, clinging to him. His kiss destroyed all the barriers she'd erected. His kiss mocked her intentions to make her career her focus, to forgo any relationship with a man.

When he pulled back, the tight band of his embrace loosening then dropping away, she wanted to stop him. She wanted to explore the feelings he'd awakened in her, but even she heard Gus returning. His whistling, which seemed out of character for the old man, alerted her to the fact he'd probably witnessed their kiss and decided to announce his rrival. Hawke further increased the distance between them y hobbling to his backpack and kneeling.

Glimpsing the rocks about her, Kit moved away from the rea as Gus rounded a large boulder, a grin on his weath- red face for a few seconds until he presented his usual tolid expression. Kit blushed and looked toward Hawke. He owned several aspirins with a swig of water.

"What happened?" Gus asked, squatting next to his ephew.

"Some falling rocks. One hit me on my back, another on ny thigh but I'm okay."

"Do we go back?" Gus pinned him with a sharp look.

Waiting the brief moment for Hawke to answer, Kit held er breath. If he needed to leave, she would in a heartbeat. he never wanted to be responsible for another person's ain ever again. Her older sister nearly died because of her oolishness, and that was something that still haunted her.

"No, we're almost there." Hawke stood and peered at her, is gaze softening. "I didn't come all this way for nothing."

"We'll rest for a few hours." Gus settled himself under n overhang and closed his eyes.

Kit started to ask why, but Hawke said, "It's not a good hing to travel during the hottest part of the day even if it's nly the middle of May. We'll wait until the sun starts its lescent behind that mesa." He pointed toward the western orizon.

"How far are the ruins?"

"At the far end. Another ten hours of hiking."

"Then we'll be camping overnight in Desolation Can- von?"

"Yes."

She'd known they would be gone possibly up to a week and would have to camp out, but now that she was here she could see why the place was named Desolation Canyon. A lone hawk had been the only creature she'd seen since nearing the entrance. The barren, stark landscape reinforced its isolation. There probably wasn't another human for miles.

He should be dead!

The Guardian drew back from the edge of the cliff. His gaze fell on his rifle, and he reconsidered using it. He rolled away from the weapon and stared up at the turquoise sky, following a hawk circling above him.

As much as he would just like to shoot Lonechief and put an end to all this, he couldn't, now that he had calmed down and thought it through logically. Two outright murders in the past few years, so closely connected to Kit, might look suspicious. Although Lonechief deserved nothing short of death, he couldn't risk involving Kit in an investigation now, since he was so much a part of her life. Last time the police had focused on Gregory, but they might not this time. Besides, if he killed Hawke, he would also have to shoot the old man. That left Kit trying to make it back on her own. She might not make it.

No, it had to be an accident, and this wasn't the place for one. Following them down the canyon would expose him. He'd wait and take care of the guide later on his turf, not Hawke's.

NINE

A cry pierced Kit's slumber the next morning, luring her toward wakefulness. Exhaustion squashed that desire, and she sank back into sleep, snuggling into the cocoon of warmth. But when she rolled over, something sharp pricked her arm. Her eyes snapped open. In the gray of dawn, she discovered herself beside a prickly pear cactus.

She scooted away, glancing toward where Hawke and Gus had bedded down for the night. The old man's sleeping bag was empty. Hawke wrestled with his as if he were fighting someone off. A moan rang through the air.

She scrambled to her feet and hurried toward him. Was he hurt worse than he'd let on yesterday? Kneeling next to him, she touched his arm.

His eyes flew open, sweat streaming off his face. "What's wrong?" Tension threaded through his question as he struggled to sit up.

"Nothing. I was worried something was wrong with you. Are you okay?"

"I'm fine." But his eyes clouded with the same tension she'd heard in his voice.

"Your uncle is gone." Concerned for Hawke, Kit sat beside him.

"He'll be back. He likes to spend time alone, especially early in the morning." Hawke kicked off the top of the bag and drew his knees to his chest, as though he needed time to collect himself. "Even when I come to visit, he goes off by himself."

After yesterday she felt a connection to Hawke. He was no longer her guide but a friend. Scanning the barren terrain, she wondered who had tramped where she had in the canyon hundreds of years ago. Soon she would know if her theory was correct—if the Spanish lieutenant under Coronado and his party had passed through here.

"I'm not used to sleeping on the hard ground, either. After this I'll appreciate my soft mattress." Kit shifted, and her stiff muscles protested. Wincing, she massaged her calf.

Hawke gave her a puzzled look.

"I figured the way you were tossing about the hard ground this isn't something you are used to, either."

"I've camped out a lot. Personally I wouldn't know what to do with a soft bed."

"I just assumed your sleeping problem was because of that. What was wrong?"

The hard set to his features matched the harsh terrain. "Too many bad memories. I should have realized this place would bring them back in full force."

"I know what you mean. I've had the same nightmare for several years," she said before she could censor what came out of her mouth.

"Nightmare? What deep, dark secret could you possibly have?"

"Everyone has secrets, even me. See, I'm not as boring as you thought." Her tone flippant, she hoped he would drop the subject because she should never have said anything. There were few she shared her past with.

"I never thought you were boring." He chuckled. "You're many things but not that. What secret keeps you up at night?" His gaze snared hers.

Beneath the gleam in his eyes, she saw the connection again, instantly traversing the short distance between them to bind her to him. He'd suffered as she had. He would know what it meant to lose a loved one. Maybe he would understand the conflicting emotions she experienced.

"I was engaged a few years back." She dragged her regard from him and stared out into the dawn with its shadows lurking in rocky crevices and alcoves. "I thought I was in love and on top of the world. My career was just starting, and I had a man who I wanted to share the rest of my life with." She paused, unaccustomed to talking about Gregory.

"I hear a 'but' in your voice. What happened?"

She slanted a glance toward Hawke. Although his expression was serious, there was something in his look that strengthened the bond between them. "He was murdered."

"Murdered!" Hawke grew taut, his hands curling into balls.

"Killed at the altar as I walked down the aisle on our wedding day."

Hawke sucked in a deep breath. "He was the one you told me about earlier."

"Yes." She remembered how close she had come to telling him about Gregory then. "But on top of all that, he wasn't the man I thought he was. He had a girlfriend in another city who he was still carrying on with, and he had gambling debts. Large ones that would have taken years for him to pay off." She shrugged, although her feelings were anything but nonchalant. "I guess he needed a lot of money since he was living a double life. I'd even loaned him some, which I never saw again. I didn't know I was feeding his addiction."

"Did the police find the murderer?"

"No, but they think it was connected to his gambling. He was associated with some unsavory people." She laced her fingers together in her lap. "At first I thought witnessing his death was the worse thing about it." Looking at Hawke, she tightened her grip. "But I'm not so sure that was. When I discovered the depth of his betrayal, I nearly fell apart." Tears welled into her eyes, blurring her image of him. "That was when I decided I was better off concentrating on my career. That's what I've been doing for the past two years."

Hawke grazed his thumb across her cheek, wiping away a tear that had rolled down her face. "One bad relationship isn't uncommon. You shouldn't be so hard on yourself."

"The worst part is that there was a small bit of time where I was relieved that Gregory was killed before I'd married him." More wet tracks coursed down her cheeks. She swiped them away, but they were instantly replaced with others. "I felt so guilty about that. Still do. No matter what Gregory did to me, he didn't deserve to die like that."

Hawke covered her hands with his and hauled her to his side. Slipping his arm around her, he pressed her against him. A tremor flowed through her.

"After Gregory, I came to the conclusion that I'm no good with relationships."

"I wouldn't say that. I get the impression you have a whole network of friends."

And you've made it clear you aren't in that network. Just my guide. "I'm not talking about friendship relationships. I'm talking about a man/woman one. Happily ever after."

He tensed. "Marriage is a lot of hard work."

"Hard work for me has never been a problem. I really shouldn't be surprised about my lack of ability to choose the right man for myself. My father wasn't exactly the best example, and he took every opportunity to let me know I was worthless as a daughter." She heard the words she uttered as though another person had said them. She never talked about her dad, and here she'd gone and told Hawke. *Why him, Lord?*

The comforting feel of Hawke's hand as he rubbed it up and down her arm conveyed more support than she'd ever received from her father. Although Hawke was silent, his presence seemed to say, *Let go of the past.*

"My dad loved alcohol more than his family, and as I got older, it got worse. Finally he left us, but my sister and I had already grown up in a household full of anger and fear."

"How old were you when he left?"

"Twelve. We never heard from him again."

"I'm sorry, but you were better off without him."

"I know." She twisted toward Hawke to look at him. "I've never told anyone that last part. I shouldn't have..." She tried to draw away.

His embrace tightened. "I'm glad you shared that with me. It helps sometimes to talk about it. I believe you told me that one time."

"Then tell me about your nightmare."

He tensed, but his arm remained around her shoulders.

The silence between them lengthened as the day brightened.

Kit started to take back her request when he finally said, "I was so eager to show Pamela the countryside that I loved and wanted to return to. Now I wished I had never come home to visit even though I wasn't happy living in New York City. At least she would still be alive today."

His pain tore at her composure. She needed to comfort as he had. She took his hand within hers and waited for him to continue.

"The ground by the edge of the cliff gave way. I couldn't stop her from falling."

"Sometimes there's nothing we can do." She remembered holding Gregory in her arms, feeling his last rattling breath, willing life back into him.

"You don't understand. I managed to get a grip on a couple of her fingers, but it wasn't enough. I couldn't hoist her up. I'd gone soft living in New York, working all the time in an office. She fell to her death seconds before I could get a better grasp on her hand. The look of terror on her face will stay with me always."

As would the look of total love and devotion in Gregory's, which she now knew was a lie. She clamped her teeth so tightly her neck muscles ached with the strain.

Emotions electrified the air, not a sound resonated through the quiet.

"I know you, Hawke. You did what you could. It was an accident."

"We'd stopped to enjoy the view. While dropping my backpack, I turned away from her. If I hadn't…" He stared at the ground, his features as stark as the landscape. "When I turned back, she'd moved too close to the edge. I started toward her, opening my mouth to tell her to come forward. I know how precarious the edge can be. The words never left my lips. It happened so fast all I could do was react, but I've kept going over and over the sequence in my head. Could I have done something else to save her?"

Beneath her palm his hand shook. "Does beating yourself up over something you couldn't stop make you feel better?"

He tensed, jerked away and vaulted to his feet. Glaring down at her, he curled his fingers into fists. "Is this your way of consoling someone?"

"Is that what you want? I know firsthand it doesn't make you feel better." Slowly she stood, her muscles screaming with the exertion. "Pamela died four years ago, and you haven't been able to move on because you blame yourself for something you didn't cause."

"I shouldn't have brought her. She didn't understand the dangers. I should—"

Kit held up her hand. "Stop. Quit coming up with reasons you should blame yourself. It won't bring your wife back. Ask yourself instead would she have wanted you to retreat from life because of what happened? Why are you trying to carry it all on your shoulders? Let the Lord help you. If you let Him, He'll walk beside you and take the burden from you."

"You don't understand!" Arms stiff at his sides, Hawke flexed his hands.

"I do. More than you know. You think I didn't go through the blame stage after Gregory's death. I could have loaned him more money. Then maybe he could have paid off his gambling debts and not been murdered that day. You don't think I didn't feel guilty when I listened to my mother cry herself to sleep because my father had left her even though he never paid attention to her and barely paid the bills. I was glad he was gone. We were free. Yes, it was hard for us, but I didn't have to cower and hide from him when he started drinking."

His glare homed in on her face. "What happened with you was different."

"Not really. My guilt did a number on me for a long time

even after I discovered Gregory had another girlfriend. Thankfully I had a friend knock some sense into me. He convinced me to turn my troubles over to the Lord. Once I did, it made all the difference in the world. It can for you, too."

With a violent shake of his head, Hawke pivoted and stalked off. As he passed his uncle returning to the campsite, he murmured something to him, then kept going while the old man shuffled toward her.

"My nephew can be stubborn."

"I've discovered that." She finger-combed her hair, then decided to search for the brush she'd brought.

"I hope he listens to you. I tried telling him he couldn't stop what happened. Some things are inevitable, like the sun rising each day." He grinned. "That's why I decided to show you the way into the canyon."

"He has to want to let go."

"He does. He just doesn't know it yet." Gus ambled to his sleeping bag and rolled it up.

A few minutes later Hawke strolled back into camp, a blank expression on his face as though they hadn't shared any painful memories. "We need to get going. We'll eat while walking."

His hurried movements spoke of a man running from his past. Having dealt with her emotions surrounding Gregory and his betrayal, the guilt over her father, she knew Hawke wasn't ready, might never be. Some memories were easier to keep buried because examining them might reveal too much.

The Guardian sat in Kit's home among her possessions. Her new alarm code hadn't foiled him, since he'd had the foresight to install cameras at the two entrances of her house. Didn't she know he was too smart for her to do that?

He didn't like the fact he didn't know what she was doing. That bothered him more than her trying to keep him out of her place. He needed to protect her, and yet he couldn't because she was inaccessible in the canyon.

Lonechief kissed her! He'd tried to erase that image from his mind. He couldn't.

His anger boiled to the surface, having festered for a day since he'd hiked back to civilization. What was Kit doing? What was Lonechief doing?

He's a murderer. Doesn't she see that? She's too good for him. Again the picture of her locked in Lonechief's embrace seared even more into his thoughts.

Foolish woman. Putting herself in harm's way. Making him have to do things he didn't want to.

The Guardian shot to his feet, fury engulfing him. He paced from one end of her bedroom to the other. Finally he couldn't contain his rage. He thrust open her closet and began yanking her clothes from the hangers.

Although Kit wore a wide-brimmed hat while they hiked farther into the canyon, her face felt on fire, as if the sun seared through the canvas material to scorch her skin. She sought any bit of shade there was. With the heat draining her energy, Kit trudged forward, forcing herself to keep going.

Not far ahead, a sheer cliff, rising hundreds of feet into the air, jutted upward in grandeur. The sun striking its rocky, red surface made it appear as though it was on fire, too. Bare, with little growing on it, she knew they had reached their destination because Coronado's lieutenant had described encountering a wall of flames. Some people had thought that had been the talk of a deranged man, but she now knew this was what he'd meant.

Scanning the area at the end of a small canyon off the main one, she certainly understood why no one came this way. She'd had to squeeze through another narrow passage, then climb over mounds of boulders littering the ground. Hawke had told her that it had been an ancient rockslide.

Hawke came to her side and pointed. "Around this bend are the ruins of the mission."

Gus disappeared ahead.

"This has got to be it." Kit quickened her steps, eager to investigate while there was daylight. "Why else build a mission in the middle of nowhere unless there was a good reason."

"And you think gold is the reason?" Hawke, a pace behind her, asked.

"As you've told me, it's a powerful motivator."

Kit rounded the bend and halted. Mounds of adobe brick, crumbling walls and vegetation growing among the ruins spread before her. Moving slowly forward, she could hardly believe this chaos at one time was a Spanish mission. And yet on closer examination, she could make out part of the perimeter of the structure that had stood in the canyon hundreds of years ago.

"The elements haven't been too kind to the mission," she murmured almost to herself, but Hawke heard even though he was yards away.

"Nothing out here survives for long if it isn't taken care of. The Spanish didn't stay."

"In Lieutenant Diego's papers he didn't talk about why he left." Kit made a full circle. "But looking at the location of the mission, I can't imagine it being very accessible, especially back in the 1500s. Which poses the question, why did they build a mission here unless he felt the City of Gold was nearby?"

"Questions you may never have answers for." Hawke covered the space between them.

"They didn't stay more than two years. An Indian uprising drove them out of here."

"I'm surprised they would stay that long. The isolation and relentless heat could drive a lot of men mad."

"Exactly. So what kept an ambitious man like Lieutenant Diego in a place forsaken by most?"

"The City of Gold?"

"I'm hoping so." Kit searched the ruins. "Where's Gus?"

"He's scouting the area. Since we'll be staying the night, he'll find the best camping place."

"Did he know about the mission?"

"Yes. There isn't anything around here he doesn't know about." He swept his arm wide, indicating the terrain. "This has been his playground all his life."

"A big one," Kit said with a laugh.

"He didn't know the mission's history. Nothing was passed down about it, which is strange in itself. This canyon system isn't taboo, but most stay away from here. The Spaniards may have named this Desolation Canyon, but my people have always referred to it as Forsaken Canyon."

Glancing toward the sun beginning its descent, Kit shrugged out of her backpack. "I'd better use what time I have." She rummaged in her belongings until she withdrew her digital camera.

"Be careful. Rattlesnakes are here as well as at Black Horse Pass."

"Thanks for the warning." She grimaced.

She began by walking around the perimeter to get a feel for the mission's size and to snap pictures. Small, its back wall abutted the canyon bluff. When she knelt in its shade, she discovered the wall was the cliff. Why? The Indians used the land as part of their structures, but usually the Spanish didn't.

"You said there's evidence Indian ruins are beneath the mission. Where?" Kit asked Hawke as he approached her.

He pointed to an area that had washed away. "Those are pot shards. Indian. Not anything the Spanish would have made."

Kit touched the largest piece and noticed faint geometric symbols on it.

"Where the ground has eroded there is evidence all over this site of the Indians' presence." Hawke indicated a couple of other places.

Awed by the ancient artifact, Kit put the shard back exactly how she'd found it. She wasn't an archaeologist and didn't want to disturb the ruins any more than she needed, especially if this was where the Lost City of Gold was.

"Where do you think the altar and sanctuary were located in this?" Kit stood and dusted off her knees, taking a photo of the piece of pottery lying on the ground.

"If it's a typical mission, it should be there." Rising, he indicated a mound of adobe bricks several feet away. "But as you stated this isn't a typical mission. I didn't find any evidence there." He twisted around and walked a few steps to the cliff. "I think they used this slab as an altar."

The stone jutted out of the bluff's facade. Examining it, Kit noticed its surface had been smoothed, almost leveled. Strange, if that was the altar. What else didn't quite add up?

Eager to investigate the site, Kit surveyed the rest of the deteriorated mission, and recorded it with her camera. With Hawke not far from her, she maneuvered around collapsed piles to bring herself to what she thought was the middle of the Spanish structure.

"This was definitely one of their smaller missions, but considering its isolation I can understand why. What I found, though, was that the army that accompanied Diego was large. For this kind of mission that's unusual. Why did he volunteer to establish a mission here?" Kit spread her arms wide. "Why such an out-of-the-way place? And why the large army of soldiers?"

"You think they were protecting a find?"

Kit glanced at Hawke slightly behind her. "Maybe."

"If the Lost City of Gold is nearby, then why doesn't the whole world know?"

"Because I think the lieutenant kept it a secret from the Spanish government, his own private stash."

"Wouldn't that be difficult to hide when he returned to Spain?"

"That's the interesting part. He died a pauper not long after he returned, and he was the only person who left this canyon alive. Some thought he was a raving madman who had been in the desert too long. The name Desolation Canyon came from him."

"You think he found and lost the City of Gold?"

Kit nodded.

"Then all this might only be a staging area for a hunt, and the city is nowhere near here."

"Possibly. But I have to know for sure." She swung around. "I just had a thought. What happened to all the men with Diego? Were there any bones or skeletons found here over the years?"

"Not that I know of. At least not in this century. What did Diego say in his writings?" Frowning, Hawke looked around him.

"The only thing he wrote was that some of his men died of an unknown disease. There wasn't anything else."

Her curiosity aroused, Kit turned back in the direction of the cliff wall with the altar. She stepped forward, intending to go back and take a closer look. Nothing added up. Something wasn't right. This was the place. She could feel it.

Scaling over some rubble, in her haste she put her foot in a crevice. She tugged but was trapped. Staring down, she yanked up hard on her leg. The fissure released its hold, and she fell back, hitting the earth with a bone-wrenching impact. Suddenly the ground beneath her gave away. She plummeted.

"Hawke!" she screamed.

TEN

Kit's scream lacerated Hawke like a knife. He dived toward her, trying desperately to grab her. His fingers clutched air. Scrambling on all fours, he plunged his arm into the black rift in the earth, opening and closing his hand to grasp any part of Kit. Nothing.

Like Pamela. Why, Lord? Why again?

Inching forward, his heartbeat booming in his ears, he stuck his head over the hole. Stale, musky air, embellished with a dank, earthy scent, accosted his nostrils. "Kit! Kit, are you okay?"

Please, Lord, let her be alive.

Kit slipped downward in a hail of dirt. She tried to yell again, but soil instantly poured into her mouth. She spat the filth out, its metallic, foul taste choking her.

Crashing against something immovable, she bounced off and continued to descend. Pain radiated outward from the contact, threatening to swamp her. Blackness engulfed her.

"Kit. Answer me. Please."

Still nothing from the dark gap.

Hawke leaped to his feet and clambered over mounds of

decaying mission. When he reached his backpack, he tore it open and dumped its contents on the ground. Snatching up his coil of rope and flashlight, he hurried back to the orifice that had swallowed Kit while his uncle ran toward him.

As Hawke searched for somewhere to tie the rope, he shouted over and over, "Kit, are you okay?"

Kit banged into another stationary object and clutched it to still her descent. The collision knocked the breath out of her. Stars burst before her eyes. Her lungs burned.

Tightening her grip around what felt like a stone pillar, she cleaved to it with the last of her strength. She inhaled a deep breath of the dusty air, trying to ease the constriction about her chest. But instead coughs seized her.

"Kit, are you okay?"

She heard Hawke's voice through the ringing in her ears and focused on the deep, gruff sound of it.

"Yes." She wasn't sure if she said the word aloud or not. Her head spun from the dizzying drop.

"Hang on. I'm coming to get you."

Hang on? She hoped she could.

The faint sunlight from above didn't illuminate the area around her. Everywhere she looked darkness greeted her. The muscles in her arms quivered from fatigue. More coughs further abused her body. Again she tried to rid her mouth and throat of the taste of earth, but it lingered.

Father, I need You. Help! Give me strength.

His presence surrounded her in a calming cloak. Closing her eyes, she basked in His love and power. Hawke would save her. He would be the Lord's instrument.

Slowly she took deep breaths and filled her lungs, easing

the racing of her heart. She locked her fingers together to secure her hold on the pillar. Using her right leg, she felt the spot around her. When her foot encountered a drop-off, she pulled it back and clung tighter to the stone.

Gradually the glow from above grew and came nearer. She concentrated on Hawke lowering himself, confident he could get her out of this situation safely.

As the light invaded her dark world, she surveyed the ledge she was on. Beyond it, the ebony shroud still reigned. *What is this? A cave below the mission?*

The stuffy air, cooler than what was above ground, hinted at a mystery beyond. The fact Hawke's flashlight couldn't penetrate the black enough for her to make out her surroundings reinforced her conviction this was a cave or a mine, perhaps a large one. Was this connected to the Lost City of Gold?

Had the Indians known about it? Probably. Their command of their domain had been impressive. How about the Spanish conquerors? So many questions flew through her mind that her sore muscles diminished in importance.

"Kit?"

"I'm over here." She peered toward Hawke, only yards above her and to the right.

He swung his flashlight in her direction. Its rays inched toward her and finally touched her. "Don't move. You're on a small ledge."

"I know. I'm not going anywhere." She fixed her gaze on Hawke, relieved to see him.

If she were interested in a relationship, he would be perfect—caring, intriguing, complicated, never dull. Whoa! A relationship! Where had that thought come from?

The light bathed her in the knowledge that he was so close

she could almost touch him. Now that she saw how small the shelf was, she was amazed that she had ended up on it. She scooted closer to the pillar, where it was wider, to give him room.

Dangling from the rope, Hawke hovered above her for a long moment as he swept his flashlight around, taking note of the stone lip jutting out from an escarpment. His left booted foot brushed the platform first, quickly followed by his right. With his hands still gripping his line, he inched closer to her.

Her breath trapped in her lungs, she gave him as much space as possible. Now that she could see where she was, she could let go of the pillar, but it had become her safety net, like Hawke's rope around him.

Next to her, he squatted against the wall. His smile warmed her. "I have this feeling you'll want to explore what you've discovered."

The sound of his voice tingled down her spine. "You know me too well."

"Not nearly enough." He reached out and caressed her cheek with an unsteady hand.

His husky words mesmerized her. The glint in his eyes charged the space between them as though an electrical storm raged below ground.

Her already dry mouth became parched. The slowing beat of her pulse increased its speed. On a ledge suspended above an unknown entity, she realized she was in deep trouble, not just physically but emotionally. She was afraid he already had her heart.

"I thought you were gone," Hawke said, his voice thick with torment. "Your voice was music to my ears."

The implications of his words crumbled all her defenses.

He'd been made to go through what had happened to his wife all over again. That would be enough to crush most people, but he held himself together and had rescued her.

"Do you remember what I taught you about climbing on that mesa?"

She nodded, newfound feelings clogging her throat. She didn't want to fall in love. That always meant pain. The two emotions had always gone together in her life, first with her father and later with Terry and Gregory. Somehow she had to shore up the wall around her heart, or she was going to be hurt deeply before this trip was over.

"We'll take it slow and easy. Gus is up there, making sure the rope doesn't come loose."

"You would have to say that. Is there a possibility of that?"

"Always plan for every possibility and then you aren't surprised."

"You planned for this?"

He grinned, an endearing gesture. "Well, not exactly this, but I thought we might have to do some climbing—just not below ground. I wish I'd brought more appropriate equipment to explore a cave."

"So you didn't know there was one here?"

"No, that was a surprise." He took a rope and tied it around her waist. "Where are you hurt?"

"Everywhere."

"Do you think anything's broken?"

Kit moved a little to see. "No, just bruises and abrasions."

"Okay." He finished making a harness for her, then started inching back to the part of the shelf directly under the hole.

"Where are you going?" she asked without thinking.

"I'm going up first. Then Gus and I will haul you up."

"I can climb."

"I want to make sure you're all right. The less you do the better." He gave her a second flashlight. "When I leave, come over here. Can you do that?"

"Sure," she murmured with more bravado than she really felt. She'd never been afraid of heights, but looking down into blackness wasn't going on her Favorite Things To Do list.

"I won't be far away." He began his ascent. "Remember we are connected by the rope. I'll tug on it when I'm ready to pull you up. You jerk it when you're ready."

We are connected. She couldn't get those words out of her mind. They radiated a warm fuzzy feeling down her length.

As his light grew farther away, Kit shone hers into that dark void beyond her. Once her beam grazed a wall where she managed to see some kind of drawing. Otherwise the flashlight wasn't strong enough to reveal much.

Excitement built while she studied the bold black lines and wished again she was an archaeologist and knew their meaning. This might be exactly what she was looking for. If so, no wonder the Lost City of Gold wasn't ever found. It was below ground, part of a hidden cave system.

The tug on her line prompted her to sidle toward the other end of the ledge. She almost hated to leave. When she positioned herself where Hawke had been only minutes before, she yanked her rope. Her ascent took longer than her descent but didn't hurt nearly as much. The back of her hand scraped the side of the wall on a sharp rock that she was glad she hadn't encountered on the way down.

When she reached the top, Hawke bent over and lifted her from the hole while Gus held the line. He swung her to the ground but didn't release his hold. Locked in his arms, he gave her a quick kiss that did more to disrupt her heartbeat than the plunge into the abyss. She tightened her arms around him, wanting to explore this more.

A sound, a rather loud one for Gus, caused Hawke to set Kit a few feet from him. A flush tinted his tanned features, and if the heat of her cheeks was any indication, she blushed even more than he did when she realized Gus stood near.

"Gus has set up camp nearby. I'd like to treat your cuts." He picked up a canteen and gave it to her.

As she sipped the water, Kit peered around Hawke and watched Gus shuffling toward a place in a protected part of the cliff. "I can take care of myself." In the fading light of the day she was determined to get some kind of handle on her emotions concerning Hawke, and if he had to touch her over and over while he cleaned her abrasions, she would be in trouble.

"Humor me."

She didn't want to argue so she kept her mouth shut, but when he approached her with the first-aid kit, she took it from him. "At least I know how to do this. However, thanks for offering."

She limped toward her bedding and sat, refusing to look his way. She didn't need to, because she felt the drill of his gaze boring a hole into her.

The next morning when her feet touched the floor of the cave for the first time, a thrill shot through Kit, and for a moment the feeling eclipsed her many aches. Nothing would stop her from exploring her discovery.

They each had their flashlight with extra batteries, which afforded them some illumination, but not nearly enough to see everything at once. It would have been nice to have their hands free, their source of light on some helmets, but caving wasn't something Hawke had planned for. They'd even argued briefly about going back to his ranch to get everything they needed. She'd pointed out there might be nothing down here but a big hole, that they should check it out before going to that kind of trouble. Reluctantly Hawke had agreed.

She'd wanted to come right back down yesterday, even though she ached from the fall, but Hawke had made her wait until this morning. She might as well, though, have gone back under the ground immediately because she didn't get any sleep. Her mind had refused to shut down with all the possibilities with the discovery of the cave beneath the mission.

"Where should we begin?" she asked Hawke, who was the last to descend from the top.

"I'd rather you not go off by yourself. You and I will stick together."

"But..."

"Yes?" Hawke arched an eyebrow.

Following Gus's beam off to the side of her about ten yards, she swallowed her protest. Hawke was right. She wasn't as equipped to handle an emergency down here as his uncle. Although she hated to admit it, she had to acknowledge her limitations in a world she wasn't as familiar with as these two men.

"Nothing," she said with a shrug.

"Hawke, come here. You need to see this."

Gus's voice from the darkness sounded excited, not the usually staunch man Kit had come to know.

"He's found something." Kit stepped forward, but Hawke halted her progress.

"Shine your flashlight on the area you'll be walking. Make sure it's safe. We don't know what to expect. We could have another cave-in and I don't think your body could go through another fall like yesterday."

Kit trailed after Hawke, trying not to limp too much or show any indication that there weren't too many places that didn't hurt when she moved. There was no way she would have stayed back. Whatever was here was her find.

Gus shone his light on a stone near an opening in the rocks. "Not good." Faded black lines forming a picture of a feathered serpent that had a grip on a man, strangling him, carved a scowl in the old man's weathered face.

"What do you mean?" Kit stepped forward and knelt to examine the drawing more closely.

"It's a warning of danger." Gus gestured toward the petroglyph. "The serpent is Quetzalcoatl, an Aztec god."

"I can't let this stop me." Kit glanced up at Hawke then Gus.

Hawke chuckled. "I think Zach rubbed off on you."

Gus moved his beam toward the opening in the rocks. "She sounds like Zach's grandfather. We'll keep going." The old man slipped through the slit in the wall.

"Stay right behind me." Hawke quickly followed his uncle. *Father, please protect us.*

Kit hurried forward, the beating of her heart increasing as she neared the dark crevice and disappeared into it. Hemmed in, the brush of the cool stone touching both her sides, she kept her attention glued on Hawke, only two feet in front of her. After several twisting turns, the path widened until she had to stretch her arms out to graze each wall.

The sound of rushing water grew louder the farther Kit went. *It's nothing. Water forms caves. It shouldn't come as a surprise.* Although she repeated those sentences over and over, Kit couldn't stop the fear from her childhood engulfing her in a cold sweat.

The passageway slanted downward while the roar of water intensified. Beads of perspiration rolled into her eyes, stinging them. She wiped her free arm across her forehead.

Gus paused next to another petroglyph and examined it for a moment before starting forward again. Kit came up to Hawke while he inspected the drawing of a monster, a combination of a bear, mountain lion and an unknown animal, driving a spear through a man's heart.

"Do you think this is another warning?" Kit asked, glad none of the dread she was experiencing cut through her question.

"Yes. I want to take you back."

"No!" She gripped him, forcing him to look at her. "I won't break. I can do this. I've worked years to get here."

"There may be nothing here. Probably isn't anything."

His muscles beneath her palm tensed. She moved into his personal space, the distance between them mere inches, and stared up into his granite-set face. "I need to know. I've come too close to let a few warnings stop me. If you want to go back, then do." As she threw the challenge at him, she dropped her hand from him, severing their tie, and stepped away.

"Yeah, and leave you down here by yourself." Sarcasm oozed from each word. "I was thinking you could go back, and Gus and I could do some exploring, check everything out. Then if you must see what we found, you can come down when I determine it is safe."

"I'm going ahead with or without you," she said through gritted teeth.

"Fine." His pinpoint gaze bored into her. "Suit yourself, but I'll carry you out of here if you don't follow every direction I give you. No matter what."

She had to agree because the fierce look in his eyes told her he would do exactly that and she wouldn't be able to stop him. "Deal."

"I don't like the sound of that water. The cavern below us may be flooded, and if so, that ends our trek." He pivoted forward.

She didn't like the sound, either, but she didn't intend to tell him that. There would be a way. She felt it deep inside. She hadn't come this far to turn back.

Hawke started down the passageway toward the noise. "For all you know this so-called City of Gold could be underwater."

The vision of that brought terror to her. She hadn't thought about that. This was semiarid land, and yet she'd known that water had formed many caves in the area. Plodding after him, she placed each foot carefully on the stone path because the humidity made the rocks slippery. More sweat popped out on her forehead. Her heart continued its maddening beat.

Ahead the area opened up, and Gus was nowhere to be seen. She hurried her pace to keep up with Hawke. When she emerged from the passage, she halted at the sight before her.

A few yards away an underground river rushed past them, disappearing into the darkness. Flashes of the last time she'd been swimming, when she was eight, drenched her in even more perspiration, as if she had immersed herself in the water before her. She'd been so sure she could swim that when she tried to in the lake, she'd ignored her sister's shouts. When she went under halfway to the float, she'd realized her mistake. Later, after her father had pulled her out of the lake and revived her, she'd taken the beating without a whimper. She'd deserved that one because her sister had nearly drowned trying to save her.

Hawke touched her arm and shouted, "Stay here. I'm going to look around. I'm sure that's what Gus is doing."

Numb from the memory, she could only nod, her gaze transfixed on the river frothing past her as though it was boiling. At eight all she'd wanted to do was show off her new swimming abilities. She hadn't realized the consequences of her rash action. Her father had beaten her before, but with his drinking increasing, so did the battering until he'd walked out on her and her mother and sister.

She didn't know how long Hawke and Gus were gone. Time meant nothing as she stared at her nemesis. But when they returned, the grim expressions on their faces didn't bode well for her mission.

"This side comes to a dead end." Hawke assessed her with a probing gaze as though he could read what she had been thinking.

Kit shifted away from his sharp regard. "How about the other side?"

"Not sure. Our lights don't penetrate all the way," Hawke said while Gus strode to the edge of the river.

"Then maybe there's a way over there." She flipped her hand toward the black backdrop covering the other side.

"The only way is to cross the water and find out."

She slid her glance to the rushing stream and shuddered at the thought of submerging herself into it.

"What aren't you telling me?"

Although Hawke had lowered his voice to below a shout,

she heard him and closed her eyes for a few seconds as if that would rid her of the problem. "I haven't swum since I was eight years old."

"Why not?" He lifted her chin so she was forced to peer at him.

"It's a long story, and we don't have all day to stand around and discuss it."

"Do you know how?"

She nodded, hoping the ability was like riding a horse—that all she had to do was get back up on the animal.

"Then I'll go across and check that side out. If there's a way, then you and Gus can follow. There's no reason for all of us to get wet if there isn't."

"Sure," she mumbled, relieved that she had a reprieve and conflicted about what she wanted Hawke to find. She would either be greatly disappointed or have to face one of her worst fears. Not good prospects for her.

Lord, Your will.

Hawke shrugged out of his backpack, the only one they had brought down into the cavern, and slung it across the river. The sound of it landing was lost in the noise of the water and the thundering of her heart.

When he approached the stream, she swung away and pretended an interest in the wall near the opening they had come through. But the rock face blurred as she imagined him battling his way across. What if he was swept away to disappear into the darkness? It would be her fault. How would she live with herself? She didn't breathe decently until she heard his shout from the other side.

"I'll be back in a minute."

Finally she pivoted toward the river and picked her way to the edge where Gus stood. He kept his light trained on the far shore, so she shone hers in an area nearby, a beacon in the ebony surroundings.

Ten long minutes later Hawke appeared in the glow of her flashlight. "There's a way out of here. Kit, I want you to come first then Gus. Give him your lamp."

Like a robot, she thrust it into the old man's grasp, anything to prolong her getting into the stream. Then when she had no choice, she trudged to the lip and stared at the river as if it were hypnotizing her into submission.

"Kit. You can't walk. It's too deep for you. You'll have to swim. Are you sure you can?"

She nodded, not even positive he saw her gesture, but she couldn't say anything. Even with the high humidity, her throat jammed as if a dry rag was stuffed down it.

I can do this. I've done it before.

"Here, Gus. Tie this around Kit's waist."

She felt the old man slip some rope around her and his fingers swiftly tie a knot, securing the tether to her. But even with it about her, she shook. Hot and cold darted alternately down her length until she wasn't sure if she was burning up or freezing.

"We don't have to do this, Kit." Hawke tugged on the line. "But I've got hold of you. You'll be all right. I'm going downstream. It'll give me more time to pull you to me if I need it."

She raised her head and locked gazes with him. She had trusted her life to him when she asked him to be her guide. She would have to again if she wanted to reach her goal. Inhaling a deep, fortifying breath, she eased into the flow.

Before she could put her arms out in front to execute her first stroke, the stream swept her into its clutches. A childhood fear drenched her. She opened her mouth to yell for help and swallowed a gulp of dirty water. The river sucked her under its seething surface. She grabbed hold of the rope about her and it went slack in her grasp.

Darkness cradled him in its comforting arms. The Guardian ran through his deep-breathing exercises until the last remnants of his anger burned away.

Standing in the middle of his bedroom, he felt the fractured pieces slip back into place now that he'd had time to calm down. He was back to his old self again and knew he had to clean up all evidence of his rampage in Kit's house the day before.

Everything will be all right. It isn't time to reveal myself to her. But soon. I need to teach her to appreciate what I've done for her.

ELEVEN

Panic surged through Kit like the river around her. Desperate, she pulled on the limp rope and it tautened. Her mind swirling, she managed to grab the line with both hands and began dragging herself up. When her head broke through the surface, she gasped for air.

Hawke scrambled along the shore, hauling her toward him. The strong current made progress slower than Kit wished. The cold water, coupled with her fear, numbed her. Although she wanted to help more, terror at losing her grip kept her hands clamped around the rope.

At the edge Hawke reached down and yanked her from the stream. She clung to him, wet clothes against wet clothes. But through the chill, the warmth from his arms around her seeped into her awareness. Panting, she drew deep breaths of the stale, moisture-laden air into her lungs until her racing pulse calmed slightly.

Leaning away, she took his face within her grasp and rained kisses on it. "Thank you. Thank you. I thought I was a goner."

"I thought the same thing while I was trying to get the rope loose from the rock it caught on. I was standing downstream in case you got caught—"

She laid her fingers against his mouth to silence his rambling, so unusual for Hawke. "I'm okay."

"God answered my prayer."

"You prayed?"

"Short and to the point."

"That's wonderful."

Hawke drew back. "I'd prefer not to experience that again."

Although she couldn't really see his features well because his flashlight lay on the ground behind him, the rough huskiness of his voice emphasized his concern even more. It dwarfed the sound of the churning river behind her. He cared enough about her to talk to the Lord again. That realization warmed her as nothing else could. Later when she was back in Albuquerque, a relationship between them might not be possible, even friendship, but at least she'd shown him what the Lord could do.

"Gus, stay there. You aren't much taller than Kit, and the current is too strong. If we don't come back, you can go for help."

"Fine, boy, but you'll need her light. I'll toss it to you." When the old man threw it, he practically placed it in his nephew's grasp.

"Hopefully we won't be long. Give us an hour before you go for help."

"No. That might not be long enough," Kit said, the reality of the situation at hand pushing any thoughts of her personal life to the background.

"It'll have to do. It can't be more than sixty, sixty-five degrees, and we both are soaking wet. I don't want hypothermia to set in."

"I'm tough. I can go longer."

"We should go back now, but after what you went through to get here, I can't do that to you." His large hands framed her face, his expression tender. "But remember the deal we made. You have to do what I say."

"What if we don't find it by then, and we still have more to explore?"

"As I said this morning, we'll come back with a safer way across this river and any other equipment we might need."

"But that means leaving the canyon."

"Yep." All softness gone, Hawke disengaged, snatched up his flashlight and directed its beam toward the back wall. "I'm prepared for some things but not a prolonged exploration of a large cave system." He started toward the area illuminated. "Since we're here, let's see if it's worth coming back or if this is a dead end."

Kit wanted to say she wasn't leaving without knowing for sure, but she really didn't have any choice. She had given Hawke her word. But if he thought she would give up if they ran into a dead end, he didn't know her well. She would come back to the canyon at a later time with or without his assistance. She'd come too far just to drop it without a resolution.

The closer she neared the rock facade Hawke was interested in, the more puzzled she became. "There isn't any opening or even a slit in this."

"No—" he swung his lamp toward the ceiling "—but there's one up there."

A narrow gap taunted her with its inaccessibility. "How do you suggest we get up there?"

"We're going to climb."

Hawke threw his rope up, snagged a stone jutting out, then tested his line to make sure it was secured before starting his ascent. When he reached the ledge, he dropped the rope for her to use. She carefully picked her way up the wall, following his route and using the same indentations and crevices in the rocky surface. At the top he assisted her onto the small landing by the dark, narrow tunnel.

"This may not lead anywhere, but I think it's worth checking out." Hawke lay flat on the small recess. "I'll go first."

When all she saw were the soles of his hiking boots, she squeezed herself into the area that was about four feet wide and two feet tall. With her arms raised over her head as Hawke had done, she held her flashlight in one hand while with the other pushing herself forward inch by inch. Scooting her body across the damp, cool rocks, she glanced back at the entrance and total darkness greeted her in that direction although it was probably only a few yards to the beginning of the opening.

She'd never been afraid of the dark or tight spaces, but the farther she went, the harder it was to keep herself composed and calm. The black void behind her played with her mind. Her vivid imagination began to conjure up all kinds of bad things that could go wrong. What if they got stuck and couldn't get out? What if…

Before she hyperventilated, she called out, "Hawke, are you near the end?"

"No, and it's getting smaller."

Oh, good, just what she wanted to hear to reassure her that light, air and open spaces were near at hand.

"Wait. This may…"

Nothing. He went silent until she heard a grunt coming from him. "Are you okay?"

Several pounding heartbeats later, he answered, "Yes, this last section is tight, but I'm out. You won't have as much trouble since you're smaller."

How comforting! Not. More sweat than before poured off her. Over and over she tried to inhale a decent breath, but nothing seemed to fill her lungs, as if the tight tunnel was compressing her chest, squashing the air from her.

In the narrower part Kit turned her head to the side to keep from seeing how close the ceiling was to her nose. Slithering like a snake, she hit the area Hawke described. It was at least half a foot less than at the start. Kit felt the shimmies spread up her body, goose bumps following.

Just keep going. Don't stop.

Father, I need You.

She glanced toward the ceiling. A big mistake. Its rocky surface only an inch or two from her frightened her more than watching the river earlier. The sense of a stone coffin enveloping her drove a bolt of sheer terror through her. The scent of fear laced the air.

She came to a grinding halt as if she were nailed to the floor. Then a calm peace descended, spurring her forward again. Hands gripped hers and gently tugged her free from the granite enclosure.

A medium-size chamber, the ceiling dripping with stalactites, appeared to be a dead end until Hawke caught a glimpse of something on the far wall.

"I think I found something." He grabbed her hand and strode toward it, weaving in and out of the stalagmites that littered the floor, forming a maze. Running his hand across small waterworn ledges, he smiled. "We've got ourselves a staircase."

"Staircase? To where?" With her lamp Kit highlighted the ceiling right above them. Nothing. Then she sidled to the left and examined the area closer. Another opening?

Hawke's beam joined hers, and he even climbed up

several feet to get nearer. "This staircase is man-made, which in itself is odd."

"Look." Her light zeroed in on another series of petroglyphs near the opening. "The warning again."

"We have just enough time to check where that leads. I'll go first." He ascended to the next step. Taking the coiled rope slung over his shoulder, he tossed one end down to Kit. "Fix a harness. It'll be your safety line. These stairs are slippery and not much is left of them."

As Kit executed his instructions, she asked, "What about you? Where's your safety line?"

He ignored her comment, which didn't surprise her. This whole trip he'd looked out for her as if he was truly her bodyguard. At one time that would have upset her, but now she found it sweet. That thought took her by surprise! Hawke sweet? A laugh bubbled from her.

"What's so funny?"

"Oh, nothing." She swung her gaze to his, and her breath caught in her throat, swelling it with tender feelings she didn't want to have.

He grinned. "Somehow I feel that I'm the butt of a joke."

"Never!" Their eyes connected, an appreciative gleam sparkled in his brown depths, and her stomach flip-flopped. "But if you don't pay attention to what you're doing, I'll have to carry *you* out of here. And let me tell you, we wouldn't get too far. You've got to weigh a good eighty pounds more than me."

His chuckle floated down to her as he turned back toward the wall and continued his ascent. Two steps up, his right boot slipped off, bits of stone pelting down around her. Kit gasped as he hung from the ledge above until he found his footing.

"See," she teased while she slowed her palpitating heart. "You've got to listen to me. I know what I'm talking about."

He mumbled something she couldn't hear and proceeded to the top. When he reached the opening and positioned himself with the other end of the rope secured around him, he shouted down, "Okay, it's your turn, and watch that area where I slipped. The step is almost gone now. I wouldn't use it if you can reach the one above."

Kit started her slow climb, stretching to avoid the place he mentioned. When she arrived at the small landing and plopped down beside Hawke, she wanted to shout her triumph to the world. In the past few weeks she'd pushed herself beyond what she thought she was capable of.

"Ready?"

She smiled at Hawke. "Lead the way."

"If we don't find anything, we'll have to turn around even if there is another passage." He wiggled his larger body through the narrow opening.

Lord, You are with me at all times. I can do this.

Kit mirrored Hawke's movement, preparing herself for an even tighter squeeze than the one before.

Three feet into the tunnel, Hawke called back, "I've reached the end." A long pause, then, "Kit, I think this is it."

The awe and wonder in his voice prodded her to go faster. She ignored the wet, cold surface, the chill invading her body and the closed-in feeling threatening her. They'd discovered the City of Gold!

When she emerged from the hole, Hawke stood to the side and helped her to her feet, then shone his flashlight on the area surrounding them. A burnished gold covered the wall. She stepped closer and ran her hand along a pictograph of a deerlike animal, an Indian with feathers and a spear, and a large lizard hammered into the sheets of gold that blanketed the rock.

"A mural in gold. This is beautiful," Kit whispered, pointing her lamp farther along the side of the chamber. "What workmanship."

"I hate to say this, but we need to head back. Our time has run out." His arm brushed up against hers.

"I need more time. Can't I stay while you go tell Gus what we found?"

"By yourself?" His eyebrows shot up.

"I'm a big girl, Hawke. I can take care of myself and, believe me, there are no bad guys down here. No one has been here for hundreds of years." The staleness of the air and the eerie quiet accentuated that statement.

"All you'll have is your flashlight."

"Is there anything we can do to get more light into the cavern?"

"Let me see what I can rig up. But first, I need to let Gus know we're all right." He took a step toward the opening, then halted and peered back. "Be careful."

"All I'm going to do is examine the drawings depicted in the gold walls."

He sighed and continued forward.

When the darkness swallowed his beam, Kit scanned the ebony mantle about her. What if her flashlight died before he got back? The extra batteries were in his knapsack. The thought almost sent her after Hawke. Then she caught sight of the wall next to the opening and knew she couldn't leave yet. Risk was part of life and with the Lord by her side she was never alone.

Carefully making her way, she started for the area near the entrance and began exploring the perimeter. Fifteen minutes into her examination a noise across the cavern arrested her.

Hawke back already? No, not enough time. Then, what— A chill sheathed her as she swung in the direction of the sound.

As Hawke neared the chamber, the pitch-blackness ahead honed his senses to a razor-sharp edge. Had Kit's flashlight gone out? Or was it something else? He shouldn't have left her alone. He should have known better.

Crawling to the opening, he pushed several pieces of wood through the gap, followed by his backpack, hearing them drop on the stone floor. As he scrambled from the hole, Kit's small voice off to the side wafted to him.

"Hawke, I'm over here."

"What happened?" He moved toward her, sweeping his beam over the area. He found her sitting behind a stalagmite, her legs pressing against her chest while she hugged them to her. Her eyes huge, she stared at him, silent. Slowly relief washed over her features but not through him. "Kit, what's wrong?"

"I'm not as brave as I thought I was. I heard something and panicked for no reason." She laughed, an almost hysterical sound. "I heard something over there." Lifting her hand, she indicated the other side of the cave. "My vivid imagination came up with all kinds of things. I switched off my flashlight and crept over here to hide. I've been praying. What took you so long?"

"This." While she rose, Hawke strode back to the wood pieces, cloth wrapped around each one at the end. He removed a lighter and lit one, then handed it to Kit. "I thought these torches could give us an idea what the cavern

eld. Gus went above and found these, and I tore up a shirt
o put around them. They won't last long, but hopefully
we'll know what is here. There may even be another way
nto this chamber."

"Great. The torches make the wait worth it."

But Hawke wasn't so sure she totally believed that. There
was still little color in her face and her hand trembled as she
eld up the wood. She would never let him know, however,
now frightened she had been because she had a hard time
acknowledging her vulnerability—like him. Something else
hey had in common. He wished he would quit discovering
now alike they were. It was going to make it difficult to walk
away from her when this was over.

Before she began her search, he said, "Wait. I also
brought a blanket in my backpack. It'll help some with the
cold, but we still can't stay too long." He took it out and
draped it over her damp shoulders.

"What about you?" She huddled beneath the warmth.
"We can share."

Being that near her wasn't a good idea. "I'll be fine. Cold
doesn't bother me too much."

The smile she sent him right before she began her search
left him feeling more vulnerable than he wished. He would
be better off being a loner like Gus, not to be responsible
for another.

"Look, Hawke. I think I found the source of the noise I
heard."

He cleared his thoughts of what the future held for them.
As she examined the ground in front of her, he approached
her and stuck a piece of wood in a pile of rocks before
igniting it.

"Doesn't this look like it just fell?"

He examined the stone by his boot. "Yes." Then he swung his gaze upward. "It must have fallen from there."

"I wish I had known that an hour ago. It would have saved me a lot of grief." She released a long breath, her tense shoulders sagging.

"This is interesting. This wall isn't covered in gold sheets. I wonder why."

"Someone took them, but for some reason couldn't loot the rest of the place?"

"Possibly. Zach needs to see this. He may be able to figure out what happened here."

"Or we may never get all the answers."

"True. Let's see what else is here before we have to leave."

They began working their way around the circumference of the larger chamber. The torches brightened more of the black cave, but there were still pockets of darkness. Kit stepped around a crevice to inspect one of those places.

Skeletons, side-by-side against the wall, brought her up short. She fell to her knees. For a few seconds she worked her mouth, but no words came forth. Gulping in the musty air, she leaned closer to the bones.

"Hawke, I found something," she finally squeaked out, her voice warbling.

With his light the space glowed even more, revealing additional secrets and dozens of skeletons.

He knelt next to her, pointing toward the irons. "They were chained together." After he wedged one of his torches in a groove between two large stones, he crawled closer.

"Be careful."

"I don't think they're gonna harm me."

"Indian or Spanish?"

"Don't know." He lifted his other blazing piece of wood and inspected the back of the cranny. "I'm guessing Spanish. There's armor back here in a pile."

"So this is what happened to the others in the lieutenant's party."

"They wore out their welcome."

"Or they found the City of Gold and began looting it, forcing the Indians to attack them."

"If that's the case, I wonder where the gold they took is. How did the lieutenant escape this?"

"We may never know." Kit rose, not wanting to leave but realizing she needed to turn the site over to someone who was an expert in finding the answers to those kinds of questions. Although the blanket had helped to ward off the damp coolness that leached her body heat, it wasn't enough. A chill seeped into her bones. "Let's finish our survey. Then we'd better leave. I don't want to disturb anything any more than we already have." She hated saying that, but it was for the best. She wasn't an archaeologist.

Three-fourths of the way around the chamber Hawke paused in front of a mound of rocks spilling out from the wall. After he investigated the area, he said, "This might have been the main entrance."

"Can we go out that way if we remove some of the stones?"

"I have a feeling it was deliberately barricaded to keep others out and those guys from escaping. I think we came in the back door. Until you fell through the floor of the mission, that way had been blocked, too. The only reason you did is because the earth around here has shifted and eroded over the years, or that way might never had been found."

He quickly extinguished all the torches in the chamber, leaving only the glow from their lamps to light their way. "Let's go."

As Kit scampered into the opening to return topside, she knew she should be elated. She'd discovered the whereabouts of the Lost City of Gold most likely, but that meant soon she would have to say goodbye to Hawke. That realization disturbed her more than she cared to acknowledge.

Three days later, Hawke dropped the last of Kit's gear in her living room, the sound echoing through her quiet house.

Although exhausted from the past few weeks both mentally and physically, Kit made a full circle, taking in the comforts of civilization, everything in its familiar place. After being gone longer than she ever had from home, it was strange being here again. No dust. No heat. No creatures. And soon no Hawke.

"Kit, I'd better—"

She didn't want him to leave quite yet. "I'm glad we stopped by Zach's." Caught in the tether of his gaze, she swallowed hard to clear her throat. "And I told him about our discovery. Did you see his look?"

"He says he's a scientist, not an archaeologist, but he's got more of his grandfather in him than he thinks. I could see him making plans for an expedition while we were talking to him."

"And I'll go with him and savor every moment in the cave. I still can't believe we actually found something!"

"Believe it, Kit. Whatever it is will be a significant discovery. Those gold murals alone are priceless pieces of history. A storybook on the wall."

"Will you guide us?" she asked, barely able to contain her excitement as her find really began to sink in.

Hawke stepped back, as though it was necessary to begin separating himself from her. "No. Gus said he would. This find has intrigued my uncle. Something he didn't know about on what he considers his land."

Silence hung between them for a long moment. She'd known this moment would come when they would have to say their goodbyes, but he'd been so much a part of her life these past weeks. It would feel strange not to have him to talk to.

Her throat still tight, she finally said, "Would you like something to drink before you have to go back?"

"No, I'd better not." His gaze shifted away and lit upon her gear stacked nearby. "If you want, I can take this into your bedroom before I go."

"Sure. If I never lug a forty-pound backpack again, I'll be one happy camper. Just let me get my digital camera since I need to send Zach the pictures I took."

She bent down and dug through her gear until she located her camera. As she withdrew it, her gaze fell upon a scrap of paper under the coffee table. Curious, she picked it up.

"That's odd." Frowning, she flipped over the piece of a photo.

What looked like a blue ink line scored the small bit, part of a picture of her house. Why was it on the floor? She didn't have that many photos, and the ones she had were in her only album on an end table. She certainly hadn't torn any up that she could remember, and she only had one of her house, taken when she had moved here. She'd wanted a picture of her first home.

"What's that?" Hawke asked from the entrance into the living room after stowing her gear in her bedroom.

"Probably nothing. Just a minute." She strode to where

she kept her album and flipped through the pages until she found where the photo should have been. The blank space glared back at her. "I don't understand this."

Hawke covered the distance between them. "What are you looking at?"

"This picture is missing. I don't remember doing anything with it. And why was a piece of it on the floor? It looks like a line has been drawn through…" She scanned the living room, everything in its correct place. Okay, she was just exhausted. That was it—a paranoid holdover from before she went into the canyon. "Never mind. I'm sure it's nothing. It's not like this past month hasn't been hectic. Sometimes I can't even remember my own name."

He took the torn part of the photo and inspected it. "Maybe I should change your locks as a precaution or stay—"

"That's okay. I'll change my alarm code. If anyone tries to come in here, I'll know about it, along with half the neighborhood. And Marcus is right next door." There was no way she wanted Hawke to stay here. It would make him leaving later so much harder.

"But—"

"You aren't my bodyguard or my guide anymore, Hawke. I'm making too much out of a scrap of paper. You know how messy I can be. You've seen my office. Besides, the City of Gold has been found so there isn't much a person can do now. It's not like someone will be able to go into the canyon, find the discovery and claim it."

"Yeah, I guess you're right. I'd better go. I really should stop by the station before going home." He headed toward the foyer.

"Hawke, I can't tell you how much I appreciate you being

my guide and taking me to Desolation Canyon. All of this wouldn't have happened without you." Her earlier enthusiasm began to die at the distant look on his face.

One corner of his mouth lifted in a halfhearted gesture. "You told me on numerous occasions you would go into the canyon with or without me. What was I supposed to do?"

"Ignore the ranting of a desperate woman?"

"Ah, that's all it was. Next time—" He averted his gaze. "I mean, I wish I'd known that. I could have spent my vacation lying on a beach somewhere."

There would be no next time. She saw that in his expression, especially in his eyes. They had gone dull, flat.

That's a good thing, Kit. No messy goodbyes. He goes his way. You go yours. He'd told her he didn't want a relationship. Why did she think the time in the canyon had changed that? But no matter what she told herself, nothing felt good about this parting.

"Maybe next year you can lounge on a beach," she said to fill the tense quiet. "Personally I prefer the mountains."

"Yeah. I guess a beach and swimming kinda go together." He looked at her again. "At least they can excavate the main entrance so there'll be no more swimming across the underground river."

"It would be hard getting equipment through those small tunnels."

"Well, I'd better be going. Thanks for the…adventure."

The formality of his tone cemented his intention to leave and never see her again. *Take a risk. Tell him you care about him. That you don't want him to leave.*

He started for the front door.

Her stomach clenched. Her mouth went dry like the canyon. "Hawke, don't go yet."

He stopped but kept his back to her, his arms stiff at his sides. "I can't do this, Kit. I'm just learning to deal with Pamela's accident. How…"

Silence ate into her fragile control. She took a step toward him.

"I need to get home. I've been gone from my duties long enough." His flat voice reinforced his intention to exit her life.

Yes, his career is everything to him. Like hers. The taut set to his shoulders demanded she let him go. He didn't want to deal with any kind of emotional scene.

"Thanks again for your help," she managed to whisper.

Then he was gone from her life.

TWELVE

On top of the mesa, Hawke surveyed the valley where his house sat, having been here since before dawn because he hadn't been able to sleep.

Because of Kit.

Not long ago he and Kit had been in this very spot. Why did it feel as if it had happened an eternity ago?

Because I can't stop thinking about her. Gone less than twenty-four hours from her and she was still entrenched in his mind.

Lord, why are You tormenting me with her?

She'd made it clear her job was what she needed to focus on, and now that they're forming an expedition to Desolation Canyon to delve into what she'd discovered, her career will be taking off. She'll probably even move to a more prestigious university.

He swept his arm wide to encompass the pueblo that stretched before him. *This is my life. Where I belong. I tried New York and I didn't fit in. I won't force myself into a situation like that again. I ended up hurting the one I loved because I was unhappy.*

A vision of Kit, pushing herself to her limit in the canyon, materialized in his thoughts. Kit's words came back to mind:

"Why are you trying to carry it all on your shoulders? Let the Lord help you."

Is that what I should do? Am I using Pamela's death to retreat from life? The last time he saw Kit at her house he had been.

The guilt he'd carried for four years weighed on him as though he were dragging a boulder behind him.

"Lord, I need Your help."

A verse from Corinthians flashed across his mind and took him to his knees. "Therefore if anyone is in Christ, he is a new creature; old things have passed away; behold, all things have become new."

"Father, I don't want to feel this pain anymore. I want to live again."

More verses, learned as a child, bombarded him. Slowly the guilt shrank until suddenly the pain in his heart melted away. Kneeling at the edge of the mesa, Hawke felt as if he'd become a new man in Christ.

Thank You, Lord. Thank You for bringing Kit into my life to show me the way back to You.

A prairie falcon floated on an air current, circling the mesa, high above the valley. *Like the Lord lifts us up.*

Hawke emptied his mind of everything but the Lord's presence and let the serenity enfold him for the first time in years. The beauty of the land accentuated the power of the Lord.

All things are possible with Him by my side.

Judging by the sun's position, he knew he need to leave for work soon. He wanted to linger on the mesa, but he'd been gone too long. He needed to start now and get his life back on track. The time with Kit was in the past, like his time with Pamela.

Hawke hastened to Honor and mounted his gelding.

Twenty minutes later he dismounted and gave his horse to John to cool down. With long strides he headed toward his house for a shower.

Kit tapped her pen against the desk in her college office. The few lines she'd jotted down blended together. She had an article to write, and yet nothing came to mind—except the last time she'd seen Hawke. When they had said their goodbyes.

Her gaze fixed upon his name that she'd doodled on the side of the sheet. Why did her heart ache when she thought of never seeing him again? Why hadn't she said something to him about how she felt?

Because I'm afraid.

She wasn't meant for a serious relationship. She never wanted to be responsible for Hawke's pain, especially now that he was finally working his way through his wife's death. It had taken him four years to get to the point where he could talk about what had happened in Desolation Canyon.

She scribbled through Hawke's name. No, this was her time to devote to her career. She had it all mapped out. Even if the cave system she'd discovered turned out not to be the City of Gold that had fueled the legend, the find would guarantee her future at this college or wherever she wanted to work. That was, if she could get the paper written.

A knock at her door drew her attention. "Yes?"

Wes stuck his head into the office. "I thought that was your car in the parking lot. When did you get back?"

"Last night."

"Did you have a nice…vacation?"

"It wasn't a vacation. I was doing some research."

"For your article?" Wes came fully into the room and closed the door.

"Yes."

"So you're ready to write it?"

"Trying to and not being very successful at the moment."

"You'll do fine." His expression grew thoughtful.

For a brief moment she almost spilled everything to her colleague, then she recalled him being in her office the week before, rummaging through her belongings. Rumors of the administration looking at ways to cut operating expenses, which included professors' positions, had circulated for the past few months. Wes could be feeling the pressure to produce something newsworthy quickly in order to keep his teaching job. Time was running out for him as well as for her.

Besides, after talking with Zach this morning about forming an expedition to go to the canyon next month, she had to keep the cave system a secret, although she wanted to shout it to the world. Her time would come. The Lord was working with her on patience.

When Wes didn't say anything, Kit slid a folder on top of the paper she'd written some notes on, then pushed back her rolling chair, coming to her feet. "I'm starving. If you haven't eaten breakfast, how about getting some with me?"

Surprise flickered across the man's face. "I'd love to take you to eat except that I already have plans." He grabbed the doorknob and twisted it.

"Maybe another time, then," she murmured as Wes fled from the room.

Something wasn't right with her colleague. When things settled down, she'd try to find out what. She got the impression he'd come in here for something but had changed his mind. Why? What was going on with Wes?

With a rumble, her stomach protested her hunger. She grabbed her purse and headed for the student center to get something to eat.

The Guardian watched as Kit hurried from the history building. *She's gone. Good. I don't like not knowing what's going on with her, especially when she didn't reveal much last night when she returned. Maybe I should bug her office, too.*

He needed to keep tabs on everything with Kit now. He'd slipped up when he'd cleaned up his mess at her house. He should have seen the piece of the photo he'd taken. Thankfully she didn't think too much of it, but what if she did later?

He wasn't sure how he was going to get in with so many people around, but he would. Kit was doing things lately that weren't good for her. But at least she'd said goodbye to Lonechief last night. If she hadn't, he would have had to find a way to take care of the murderer right away, and an accident was the only thing possible. If he rushed his plans, he might mess up again. He couldn't afford to do that. He couldn't bring any more police attention to Kit or the people around her.

He fisted his hands. *Kit, why are you forcing me to do these things?*

In his bedroom, Hawke caught sight of the piece of torn photo Kit had found that he'd emptied from his pocket last night. He needed to throw it away—remove all he could of her from his life. Grabbing it, he glanced down at it.

The blue pen line mocked him. He could just make out an arm in the part of the picture he held. Probably Kit's. A tingle at his nape worried his peace of mind. Something wasn't right about this. He should have seen it yesterday.

He strode to his phone and dialed Kit's home number. She didn't answer. For a few seconds, fear nibbled at his composure. No, she could be at work already. Knowing her, she probably was. He called her at the college. She picked up on the second ring.

"Kit, this is Hawke. I need you to do something for me. Call your security company and see if anyone accessed your house while you were gone."

"No one would have, especially since I took the key from Marcus and changed the code."

"Just do it and call me right back on my cell." Hearing her voice softened his resolve to stay away from her.

"Why?"

"That piece of a picture you found bothers me, now that I've really thought about it. What if someone *had* been in your house while you were gone?"

"Why, if they were after information about the City of Gold?"

"A good question and one we'll consider if you find out someone has been."

"Hawke, I—" Alarm crept into her voice.

"Call then get back to me. You aren't alone in this."

When he hung up, he collapsed onto his bed, his hand still on the receiver. He needed a shower, but he wasn't going anywhere until he heard back from her.

What is going on?

What am I missing?

Burying his face in his hands, pressing his palms against his eyes, he tried to wipe the woman from his mind, to get back his focus, to figure out what was bothering him—had been since he had become involved with her.

Lord, I need Your help.

He emptied his mind and tuned out the world around him. Slowly pieces began to fit together. Was someone messing with Kit? Too many strange occurrences. Was Ronald Hoffman a victim of road rage? He needed to meet with the police and see what they had discovered since he'd talked to them last. He also needed to find her second guide, James Harrison. Was his disappearance connected with the search for the Lost City of Gold or was something else going on?

Remembering their conversation in the canyon about their past made his unease multiply. Her fiancé murdered in the church? Why there? Was it really because of the man's gambling debts? He would check into that case, too.

The ringing of the phone blasted through the silence. He snatched it up. "Kit?"

"Yes, and someone was in my house two times." Her voice rose to a panic level. "Twice, Hawke. Why?"

He closed his eyes, wishing he could take her into his arms and comfort her. "I don't know, but we'll figure it out. Stay at your office. I'll be there."

The second Hawke was inside Kit's office, he grabbed her, tugged her to him and kissed her. His mouth tasted of coffee and mint toothpaste. His familiar outdoorsy scent wrapped around her as his arms did. Kit wanted to drown herself in his embrace. All she'd thought about was this man who had frustrated and haunted her more than anyone should. She wanted his kiss to go on forever, but sanity wormed its way into her mind. They needed to talk.

Disengaging, she backed up. They needed space between them if they were going to talk about what was going on. "Do you think someone is still going after the City of Gold?"

The appreciative look in his eyes went neutral as though he were shutting down any emotions that had generated the kiss. "No. I'm beginning to think it might be something else."

"What?"

"Someone might be playing with your life."

"You're kidding!" She sagged back against her desk. "Why?"

He clasped her upper arms, not saying a word until she had totally centered her attention on him. "It could be any number of reasons. A stalker. Someone who is out for revenge. Someone who—"

"Revenge! I'm a scholar. A boring historian." The very idea overwhelmed her.

"Not to me. There's nothing boring about you. More has happened to me in the past month than the past several years."

His statement and look heated her cheeks. "If we rule out someone wanting revenge, then that leaves having a stalker. I would have known if someone was stalking me. I mean you're talking years. Wouldn't the person have shown himself by now? Isn't the object of stalking to pursue a person and let them know it?"

"Usually." He pivoted away, plunging his fingers through his hair. "But we can't ignore someone was in your house twice. Nothing was gone was it?"

"Not that I know of, except maybe the photo."

"Tell me about it."

"It's just me standing in front of the house the day I had my first party there."

"You were the only one in it?"

"Yes."

"Okay." Hawke kneaded his neck. "I doubt robbery was the reason that person was in your house while you were in the canyon. And remember that time Sean called to tell you about seeing someone. Sean might not have been wrong. What if there had been someone and he had a key and knew your code?"

"I don't go around handing keys out and giving people my codes." *This has to be a horrible nightmare.*

"Except Marcus, but he didn't have the new code. I even called the security company and changed my password."

"What's the code?"

"The day I moved into the house."

"There are ways to get them if someone wants them bad enough. Say someone obsessed with you."

His words chilled her to her bones. Her fingers dug into the wood of her desk, pain streaking up her arms. She wanted desperately to ignore what he was saying, but she couldn't ignore the facts.

Someone was after her.

"Okay, then what do you suggest I do?"

"Nothing. Let me handle it." He stepped away as though he needed to put some space between them in order to don his cop facade.

She closed the short distance. "No, *we* will. If this involves me, I want to know. If someone is stalking me, I want to find out who it is and put an end to it. We're talking murder, Hawke." Still stunned, she shook her head. *It can't be? Can it?* "I'm having a hard time believing that's what's going on."

"Then you and I can start right now. The sooner, the better. I want you to tell me everything about your life."

"Everything? That could take a while."

"I have the time. Let's go grab some lunch at the student union and talk."

His cocky grin made all that was happening better.

"I never turn down food."

The Guardian slammed his fist into the wall near him. Even several minutes after he'd listened to Kit and Lonechief talk, the rage boiled in his stomach.

How dare they think I'm a murderer! Lonechief is. I'll make her see that. She will appreciate me!

THIRTEEN

Putting his tray, laden with his lunch, down on a table in the student union, Hawke sat right next to Kit. "Come stay at the ranch, Kit. Mom would love to have the company, and I'd feel better if you were near. I'd sleep better, too."

"I—" His presence so near robbed her of her next thought. He was one of the few people who could invade her personal space without bothering her. Amazed at how quickly he had become a part of her life, she covered his hands with hers. "I don't know what to say."

"That's easy. Say yes." He grinned. "Besides, you need to practice climbing in case you'll need to when you go back to the canyon."

"Oh, yay. Just what I wanted to do."

"I sense sarcasm."

"Duh. Remember I'm not big into exercise."

"It's so much better when you exercise with a partner."

Partner! For a few seconds that word stunned her, but when she thought about it more, she liked it. They were partners, at least in determining if anyone was stalking her and who he was. "All this talk of working out is making me even hungrier."

As he took his dishes off the tray then placed it across from them, his laughter drifted to her. It was good hearing that. For a brief moment she had forgotten someone very likely was after her.

But all too soon reality returned when Hawke said, "Eat up, then we'll talk."

Her hands trembled as she picked up her hamburger and took a bite. Its unusual juicy flavor didn't appeal to her. Even the fries tasted like sticks of chalk. Finally she shoved away her plate with her half-eaten food. "I'm done."

Hawke finished his last bite of his barbecue sandwich, set his notepad on the table and found a pen in his pocket. "Okay, let's get down to business. Who's been in your life for the past five or six years?"

"That's a long list."

"We'll concentrate only on the men. We'll start with your closest friends, then move outward from there, since someone possibly has a copy of your key and alarm code."

"My closest?" The very thought someone she called a friend could have killed people alarmed Kit.

"You said he should have made himself known. I agree. What if he did by becoming your friend?"

"No, I don't think—" she swallowed hard "—I mean, wouldn't I know if someone was a murderer? Wouldn't there be signs of some kind?"

"If only there were in all cases, the police's job would be easier." Clicking his pen open, he poised his hand above the paper.

She slid her eyes closed and tried to keep the faces from intruding into her thoughts. The picture of Gregory's shocked expression as he was shot formed in her mind. Although she'd later found out he'd betrayed their love, she would never forget the last time she'd seen him alive. If someone murdered him because of her, she owed him to discover who that was.

Looking straight at Hawke, she said, "Okay, let's get busy. The first one is my neighbor, Marcus Perry."

"How long have you known Marcus?"

"Since I moved into my aunt's house the last year of college." Kit snapped her fingers. "Hey, he could exercise with you. He's big into it," she teased, needing to lighten the mood or all she would be able to do was focus on the fact someone was stalking her.

"I'll pass. Who else?"

"Well, there's Sean Sullivan."

"The mailman." He jotted the name down.

"I've known him almost from the beginning when I moved into my aunt's house. Almost as long as Marcus."

"Tell me about the librarian."

"Samuel?"

"Yeah. He certainly helped you with your research. Is he a close friend?"

"He's a friend, but I wouldn't say we're close." She had a lot of acquaintances, but good friends were another thing. "Wes and I have worked together for a while. I suppose I would consider him close. We have the same interests in history."

"Early American?"

"Yes. He needs to publish or perish, like me. He hasn't yet. This is his first year teaching. I suspect he's feeling the pressure, especially now with the administration reassessing all the positions."

"Do you know what he's working on?"

"Not really." Tilting her head to the side, she recalled the time she'd found Wes in her office getting a book, or so he'd said. "He's been more secretive than me."

"Another Lost City of Gold," Hawke said with a chuckle.

"Beats me. Usually he consults me. I was his advisor. That relationship has continued since he became a professor. But lately he's been different."

"Different? What do you mean?"

"Remember that time Wes was in my office right before we went into the canyon? He was acting strange, and the book he was borrowing wasn't anything that he usually was interested in."

"How far would he go to further his career?"

"Oh, I can't see…"

His sharp gaze whisked the rest of her sentence away. "Anyone is capable of killing under the right circumstances or at least going to great lengths to get what they want or think they need."

"Have you always had this jaded outlook? Is that what being a cop does?"

"For me it was being a lawyer. The firm I worked for dealt with some unsavory people. I know they have to be represented, too. I just didn't want to be that person. My wife couldn't understand that. It was a source of many arguments."

Hearing the vulnerability in his voice, Kit took his hand. "Is that the reason you wanted to come back here?"

"Maybe part of it, but I could have found a job in New York. I need the wide-open spaces, fresh air, the feel of a horse beneath me, the ability to climb a mountain and look down on the world."

"Although I wouldn't recommend scaling the side of a building, you could use a skyscraper to look down on the world."

"Nope, I'm where I belong and for the first time in four years I feel I've really come home." He laid his hand over hers. "Thanks to your stubbornness, you pushed me to put the past behind me. In the canyon I finally was able to put Pamela to rest and didn't really realize it until I got back here."

"Thank you for the…compliment. At least, I think it was one." The warmth from his touch suffused her.

"We'd better get going."

The moment of closeness vanished. Kit wiped her mouth and tossed her napkin on her empty plate. "Yes, we have work to do."

"I don't know about 'we.'"

In the process of sliding from the booth, Kit halted. "What do you mean? We agreed. We are a team."

"Most of what needs to be done right now is on the computer and making phone calls." Hawke snatched up his pad. "Is there anyone else I should include on this list?"

"Not close friends, other than my sixty-year-old minister. Do you think we should consider him?" She gritted her teeth, trying to decide how best to inform Hawke being a team meant dividing the tasks equally.

"No, but we should also consider any unusual things that have happened involving you, like Hoffman's accident."

"How about the other guide suddenly disappearing? What if something happened to him, too?"

"I'll look at these four men." He waved his pad with the names of her friends on it. "And I'll check out the two guides."

"There you go again, Hawke Lonechief." She fisted her hand at her waist. "We're a team, as in 'work together.' I'm competent on the computer. We can use my office at the college."

"No, I'm thinking we should go to my station. Get out of Albuquerque."

"Fine." She headed toward the exit. "You can make the calls."

"I can?"

His chuckle that accompanied that sentence tingled down Kit's spine. "I'm glad you're amused."

His hand on her shoulder stopped her progress. "If someone is stalking you or fixated on you for some reason we haven't been able to figure out yet, this won't be a laughing matter."

"I know." Her throat closed around those words. She scanned the area.

Am I being watched right now?

"I called James Harrison's office, and his secretary said he's back in town but can't talk because he's busy getting ready for a big trip to the Rockies. I think he's avoiding me, but he's alive at least."

Hawke stood at the door to his office with a paper in his hand. "I got the fax from the detective working on Hoffman's wreck. They found the white truck abandoned in a parking lot near the college. Paint scrapes on its side match Hoffman's car."

"That's near where I work," she murmured, sinking back in the padded chair.

"It had been stolen. They're running prints now, but nothing has come up except the owner's and a couple of his friends'."

"Who?"

Hawke read the names off. "Do you know any of them?"

Kit shook her head. "So what does this mean?"

"It means something is fishy with Hoffman's accident and makes me even more suspicious. We'll continue looking at all the men around you."

"What if it's a stranger?" She latched on to that prospect, not wanting to think it was someone she knew, especially someone she was good friends with.

"It could be. That's why I want you at the ranch. I can keep an eye on you."

"You can't be my bodyguard."

Ignoring her last statement, he continued, "You have to leave Albuquerque without letting anyone, and I mean no one, knowing where you're going."

"Someone might see me with my suitcase and say something. Marcus is always outside."

"Which makes him the top of my list, and the first person I will be checking out, especially because he had the key and code at one time."

"Marcus? It can't be him. We've been friends for—"

"I suspect everyone until proven otherwise and it's best you do, too." Hawke balled the piece of paper in his hand and tossed the wad at his trash can. "I'm also checking out why Harrison is avoiding you. Did someone pay him to get lost?"

"What if this is all for nothing? What if we are imagining danger where there isn't any?"

"Better safe than sorry. *I* won't let anyone hurt you."

"If something's going on, I can't put you or your mother in danger. If something happened to either one of you, I could never—"

With three long strides, he stopped in front of her and pulled her up and into his arms. "Don't say it. Nothing is going to happen to any of us. Besides, you don't know my mother. Evelyn Lonechief is one tough lady who can take care of herself, and she'd be the first one to tell you. If you don't come to the ranch, she'd most likely come to your house and park herself in your living room."

"Okay, I'll do it," Kit said with a laugh, realizing all along she would end up at his ranch. "You've convinced me. When do you suggest I get my things? The middle of the night?"

"No, I don't want it to look suspicious. Instead, you'll go home right now, pack a few things, using a big purse, no luggage, and leave as though you're going to the store or somewhere you'd usually go in the late afternoon."

"You're going to let me go back to Albuquerque by myself," she said in a teasing voice while cuddling closer.

"I'll be around the corner. I'll follow you there and back to the ranch. I want to make sure no one is behind you."

"Just like in the spy movies. I feel like a secret agent." Laughter tinged her voice, his warmth seeping into her, giving her a feeling of safety.

"If someone is obsessed with you, he has a way to keep track of—" He jerked away and hurried from his office, saying, "I can't believe I didn't think of this before."

"What?" Kit trailed after Hawke to the parking lot at the side where her Honda sat next to his Jeep.

He circled her vehicle, then knelt at one tire and began feeling around it. "He could have put something on your car to track your whereabouts. Probably some kind of GPS locator."

"A bug!"

"Something like that." He sent her an exasperated look. "You're much too distracting. That's my only excuse." When he reached the third tire, he produced a contraption the size of a cell phone. "Bingo." He put it back.

Stunned, she stared at Hawke for a few seconds before rushing forward. "I don't want that thing on my car." Anger gushed through her, especially when she thought of some unknown lurker nearby waiting for his chance to secure it to her car.

"I don't want the person to know it was found and run. I want to catch him. At least now there's no doubt someone is stalking you. I'll start investigating who might have bought the GPS tracking device. It'll take time, but we may be able to locate the person because of this."

"Why didn't Bud find it when he worked on my car?"

"Good question. It's not near the gas tank. But there's always the possibility it wasn't there when Bud was repairing your Honda."

"So he hasn't been tracking me for long."

"Or he took it off after disabling your car."

"Why?" Overwhelmed with all that was happening, she collapsed back against the hood. An image of a stalker watching her at Black Horse Pass where she'd been alone, miles from civilization, scared her as nothing had before. She really was in danger!

"Another good question and one I don't have an answer to. But you can be assured I'll ask when I get a hold of him." His fervent tone blazed with a chilling, unstated threat. "This only confirms what we suspected. Now I want you to pack a bag and drive to the airport. It's possible that break-in was to plant a bug in your house or even a camera, so while you're getting your things together, make it clear that you're leaving town. Come up with some excuse for the sudden departure. I don't want him to suspect we're onto him. Remember he may be hearing you as well as seeing you. I'll follow you to the airport parking lot and pick you up."

"I can't believe this is happening." Kit massaged her temples, the drumming in her head making pain shoot down her neck. The very idea that someone could have been watching her in her house numbed her with fear.

"This is a good thing." He gestured toward where he'd put back the tracking device. "It'll give me and the police time to investigate who is stalking you. I have a friend on the Albuquerque police force I'll call on the way and explain what's going on. We'll stop at his station before heading back here."

Hawke took her into his embrace, securing her against him, while bringing his mouth down on hers. So many emotions swirled through her that for a brief moment she did nothing. But his kiss managed to drive the anger, fear and shock to the background for a few precious minutes.

"I'll keep you safe," he whispered against her lips.

Kit kept repeating in her mind, *I'll keep you safe,* as she unlocked the door to her house and entered a place that no longer felt like a haven from the world. The only thing that kept her functioning halfway normally was the thought that Hawke was sitting in his Jeep around the corner and in a few minutes she would receive a call from him, their conversation planned ahead of time, a performance for anyone who might be listening.

Walking into her bedroom, she retrieved a suitcase from the top shelf of her closet and opened it on her bed. Although she knew Hawke was going to call, she jumped when the phone rang. Gasping, she splayed a hand over her heart and felt its pounding.

To be on the safe side, Kit glimpsed the number displayed on her caller ID screen, then brought the phone to her ear.

"Hello, Hawke. I thought we said our goodbyes at the pueblo."

"I couldn't let you go to your mom's without telling you to call me when you get there. Let me know how she's doing."

"I'll be going straight to the hospital. The doctors told me they've stabilized her and will be monitoring her for the next few days." She injected the right amount of worry and urgency into her voice. If someone was listening, she had to convince him she was leaving town.

"Again, I'm so sorry about the heart attack, but at least she got help right away."

"It's a good thing the hospital was able to reach me on my cell. I need to be with Mom. I'll let you know when I get there. Bye." Kit hung up, her whole body quaking.

As tears welled up into her eyes, she crumpled onto her bed and cried, loud sobs that were an unplanned part of the performance. But suddenly her whole situation crushed her resolve not to let this stalker get the best of her. She wanted to curl up into a tight ball and forget everything that was going on. She wanted to escape, really get on a plane and leave her life behind—all that she had worked for, her friends, even Hawke.

Words from Matthew drenched her in comfort: "I am with you always, to the very end of the age."

It's going to be okay. The Lord's with me.

She's leaving!

The Guardian slammed his chair back, knocking it over as he lurched to his feet. She can't leave me. She—

His raging thoughts came to an abrupt halt. "It's all right," he muttered between inhaling deep breaths. She'd be back.

She was just going to check on her mother, something any good daughter would do.

He could use the time she was away to his advantage. This could be a great opportunity to get rid of Lonechief. *An accident. It still needs to be one. It won't be easy, but I'll have a few days to follow him and figure out something.*

After he killed Lonechief, he could reveal himself to Kit and take her away from this place. He was tired of cleaning up her messes. The only way he could really protect her from danger was to keep her to himself.

FOURTEEN

She's with him! She didn't go to see her mother! She lied to me!

Lying flat on top of the mesa overlooking Lonechief's ranch, the Guardian dropped the binoculars and rolled over, staring up at the sheet of steel-gray clouds stretching as far as he could see.

After all these years of watching over her. She didn't care.

Fury clawed at his insides and burned a hole through his gut. Reeling with frustration, he clutched a rock and pummeled the binoculars until they shattered into tiny pieces.

Panting hard, he went through several relaxation techniques before he was calm enough to think rationally.

He'll pay for this. She'll *pay for this.*

Kit set her mug on the wooden railing and inhaled the clean, fresh air of a beautiful day. The sun struck the face of the mesa, coloring it red orange. A roadrunner scurried across the yard in front of Hawke's house.

Not a bad way to start a day. Kit took a sip of the wonderful coffee that Evelyn made only a few minutes ago. Its fragrance blended with the sage-scented breeze.

The door behind her opened, and Hawke tromped toward her with enough racket to wake every creature around his ranch. She smiled and turned to greet him.

"Is this loud enough for you?" He cradled his drink in one hand.

"Yep. I think you're getting the hang of letting me know when you're approaching."

"I thought I'd find you here."

"I love coming out on the porch early in the morning. It's so quiet and peaceful."

"That's until I came outside." His lips curved into a grin.

"I hope we hear back from the police soon. I'll need to call some people if I'm gone much longer, especially when I don't show up at church."

"You've only been here two days."

"You don't understand. I don't normally drop off the face of the earth without letting people know where I'm going. I have good friends who would worry about me." She sank back, half leaning, half sitting on the railing. "Well, at least, I used to think so."

"We still don't know anything for sure, and Harrison wasn't able to enlighten me about who hired him. There was no job for Harrison. At least he fared better than Hoffman, who's still in a coma."

"He deserved a few problems the way he was leaving me to go on a wild-goose chase for a job that sounded too good to be true." She chuckled. "And it wasn't true."

"This could just be the work of an acquaintance or even a stranger."

She penned him with a probing gaze. "You don't believe that, though. You think it's one of the four men you've been checking out."

"The problem is they all have something that makes me spicious." He held up one finger. "First, there's Marcus, ur ever-present neighbor, always around. He has lots of e time and plenty of money to cause things to happen."

"He has a job. He writes self-help books and manages s property."

"Which makes him computer savvy."

"But then so is Samuel. There isn't much he can't do on e computer. His world revolves around one as a research rarian." Kit shook her head. "I'm still surprised he lives block away from me on the street behind mine. He never id a word."

"Because he wanted to keep it a secret?"

"Maybe." She shrugged.

"He has a crush on you. I've seen how he looks at you."

"Our relationship has always been professional. I just don't e him wielding a gun or driving a big truck anywhere."

"The white one was found near the college, a short walk the library."

"Also not far for Wes to go, either." With each name oken, the beautiful morning evaporated around her. In its ace was terror and betrayal.

"What about the good professor snooping around your fice? I wouldn't be surprised that was bugged as well as ur house."

"We don't know if either one was."

"Too risky to find out."

"The rumor flying around the faculty grapevine is that 's in trouble with his research article, which may explain s snooping in my office."

"But would that lead to the other incidents?" Hawke pped his coffee. "I'd love to ask the young man that.

Probably not a good idea though." He shrugged, deep i
thought for a moment before continuing, "Then there's th
mailman, Sean Sullivan, trained as an army ranger to use
rifle."

"That's what soldiers are trained to do. A lot of peopl
out here know how to shoot."

"He didn't just help his sister buy the house across th
street from you, he bought it outright, a detail he neglecte
to tell you. He's the owner, not his sister."

"He's a private person. Maybe he didn't want me to kno
the extent of the help he offered his sister. Or maybe it wa
her. She's a proud woman."

"The more I delve into each of their lives, the more
feel in my gut it is one of them. Call it cop instinc
whatever you want."

"Then let's hope the police find a video of the parkin
lot that shows someone getting out of the white truck."

"Or a picture from one of the traffic cameras. We ju:
need a break. One slipup."

Opening the front door, Evelyn stuck her head ou
"Hawke, there's a call for you. It's your friend with th
Albuquerque Police Department."

"This may be it." He hurried inside and snatched up th
phone in the living room.

Kit stood by the door, listening, watching the play (
emotions across his face. Deep concentration settled over hi
features, the kind she saw when he was processing informa
tion and trying to piece it together.

"We'll be there. We'll leave right away." Hawke droppe
the receiver in its cradle and smiled. "We got a break. Th
police tracked down a videotape that shows someone exitin
the truck. The picture is grainy, but their tech people wi

ork on it. My friend hopes we can ID the person, since
ere wasn't anything in the truck."

"Thank you, Lord."

"You've got that right, Kit. We needed some of God's
tervention." After swallowing the last few swigs of his
ffee, he plucked his keys from the table by the phone.

"I can be ready in two minutes." Kit hustled into the
tchen to place her mug in the sink.

"I heard the good news." Evelyn stood at the stove,
shing an egg mixture onto a tortilla. "You two will need
eat. You can take these with you."

Kit took the breakfast burrito and ate a bite. "Delicious
usual. I'm gonna miss your cooking. Hopefully this will
d today, and you won't have me underfoot anymore."

"I've enjoyed having you here. It's like having a daughter.
lways wanted one."

Hawke's mother's words robbed Kit of speech. He had
own up in such a different home than she had. Hers had
en filled with turmoil and rage, while love and the Lord
d surrounded Hawke.

Kit cleared her clogged throat. "I'll miss you."

"I hope you won't be a stranger. You'll always be wel-
me here." Evelyn's glance strayed to her son, who had
tered the kitchen.

She quickly fixed him a burrito while Kit hastened to get
r purse and sandals on. As she'd exited the kitchen, the
preciative look Hawke had given her had curled her toes.
the hallway she paused, steadying herself against the
all.

I love him.

She couldn't deny it any longer. She'd known for a long
ne she cared for him a lot, but the emotions concerning

him went much deeper to heal all the wounds from the pas
She could put her volatile relationship with her dad behin
her. Her Father in heaven had taught her what it meant to b
unconditionally loved, that she was a worthy human being
Now looking back, she could see how her interaction wit
her dad had affected the men she had been attracted to.

*Thank you, Father, for changing my views or I woul
never have opened my heart to Hawke.*

Now all she had to do was convince a man who had shie
away from any kind of relationship since his wife's tragi
death, that they would be good together.

Father, show me the way.

As the detective brought up the taped footage, Kit steele
herself for what she might see on it. Did someone she know
betray their friendship? Her breath trapped in her lungs, sh
zoomed in on the white truck as the unknown person parke
it in a space. Seconds later, the door opened.

And Sean Sullivan climbed from the vehicle.

Although the photo wasn't sharp, she saw enough of hi
face to recognize him. But even if she hadn't, she knew hi
walk, having seen it a lot around the neighborhood as he de
livered the mail.

While she watched him stroll away from the truck as i
he'd done nothing out of the ordinary, her heart bled for th
person he'd become. *What happened? Why, Sean?* She didn
understand any of what was going on. He'd never indicate
to her he was obsessed with her to the point that he'd comm
murder. The very thought manifested a knot in her stomac
that grew until she wanted to double over in pain.

"Miss Sinclair, do you know that man?"

Words crammed her closed throat and refused to com

 it. She nodded while Hawke replied, "That's Sean Sulli-
an. He's her mailman."

"Is that correct? Are you sure it's him?" The detective's
oubled gaze skimmed over her features.

"Yes," she choked out, wishing it were a total stranger.

"Excuse me a moment." Hawke's friend rose and left the
terview room.

Hawke closed the laptop, then took her hands. His touch
rapped around her cold fingers, but nothing seemed to be
aching inside to warm her.

"Kit, everything will be over soon. This was a good thing
e discovered today."

"No!" She yanked her hands away. "It isn't. Why would
an do all those...those—" She couldn't even grasp the
agnitude of what he'd done. It didn't fit into her world or
e way he'd projected himself to her.

"We'll ask him when he's caught."

"I even—" She shook her head but couldn't rid herself
the image of Sean. "I saved his life once. I didn't think it
as that big a deal, but he did."

"What happened?" Hawke took her fingers between his
id rubbed them.

"I stopped him from stepping into the street. He was on
s mail route one of those days when I tried to take up
gging. He was fumbling with something in his bag and
dn't see the speeding car coming around the corner. The
enager missed him by only half a foot."

"Did you know him before that?"

"I saw him around the neighborhood a few times. I'd just
oved into my aunt's house. After that, he made a point to
lk with me. Then his sister bought the place across the
reet and I saw him a lot after that. I—" Her eyes wide, she

covered her mouth with her hand. "Everything change(
after that. He started going to my church. He'd asked me i
I knew a good one, and I'd told him about the one
attended."

The detective came back into the room. "Some patrolme(
are heading to his house. He isn't working today. He calle(
in sick, which he has been doing quite a bit lately accord
ing to his supervisor. Hopefully we'll catch him at home
Then they'll bring him down for questioning."

"Do we have to stay? I don't want to see him right now.
It was too much to take in. She needed time to process al
this.

"No, I think we've got what we need for the time being.

"You have my cell number." Hawke rose. "Call when th
officers bring him in. I want to be informed of what progres
you make with his interrogation."

"Will do."

Still numb, Kit allowed Hawke to guide her from the polic
station to his Jeep. She still couldn't believe the man who'
helped her get through Gregory's death and betrayal may hav
killed her fiancé. He'd seemed so sincere and caring. He'd–

Another person she had read wrong—dead wrong.

Kit sat in the Jeep and leaned against the door, her arm
folded over her chest. What was wrong with her and the me(
she chose to care about? Maybe when this was all over, sh
should go off and live by herself on top of a mountain whe(
she didn't have to deal with people or with feelings. Sh
wasn't good at it.

"Kit?"

"Hawke, I'd rather not talk about it right now."

Another ten minutes and they were on Interstate 4(
heading out of Albuquerque toward his ranch. The monote

nous ribbon of highway stretching before the Jeep lured Kit's eyes closed. She rested her head on the seat back and relished the quiet, emptying her mind of all thoughts.

The sound of Mozart's *The Marriage of Figaro* penetrated her drowsy state and jarred her fully awake. Hawke flipped his cell open and listened to the caller.

"I see. No idea where." A frown slashed across his face, his voice strained.

She tensed, gripping the door handle so tightly her hand ached. When he ended the call, she asked, "What's wrong?"

"Sean Sullivan wasn't home. It looks like he hasn't been there for a few days. He may have fled town or—"

"Gone to Florida to my mother's? Gone after me?"

"It's a possibility." He gave Kit his cell. "Call her. Have her leave her place and stay with a friend until you let her know everything is all right."

She could barely hold the phone, let alone punch the buttons for her mother's number. They had never been close, but in her own way Kit knew her mom loved her. She'd just been scared from years living with an alcoholic husband.

When she heard her mother's voice, Kit nearly broke down, all her tears suddenly coming to the surface. She couldn't cry. She didn't want to frighten her mom any more than she would by asking her to leave.

"Darling, it's good to hear from you."

"Mom, I have something I need you to do." Kit paused, not sure how to proceed. But there wasn't any way to sugarcoat her request or why she'd made it. "I need you to go to a friend's place and stay for a few days. You shouldn't go back to your house until I call you."

"Why? You're scaring me."

Welcome to my world. Kit gripped the cell phone even

tighter. "This is important. Someone may be coming to Florida looking for me and you can't be there."

There was a long silence. "Kit, what's going on?"

"This man has been stalking me and thinks I might be there with you."

The cry of alarm from the other end echoed so loudly from the cell that Hawke heard it. She took in a deep breath, Hawke's familiar scent pervading her and calming her. "Please, Mom. I have police protection, but I don't want to be worrying about you. I'll call when this is over and explain everything in detail."

"Do you promise?"

"Yes," Kit said as Hawke turned onto the paved two-lane road to the pueblo.

"What if this man comes here?"

"Leave now and you'll have nothing to worry about."

"May I?" Hawke held his hand out for his cell. When she gave it to him, he said, "Mrs. Sinclair, I'm protecting Kit. I work for the police. I'll be calling the detective in charge of the case to have him let the authorities in Florida know of the possibility that the suspect might arrive there. This will be over soon. They have an APB out on him, and if he comes there, they'll catch him." Hawke listened for a minute longer, then said, "She'll phone. Yes, you'll be at Flora's. I'll tell her. Goodbye."

"Flora's her third cousin. She lives on the other side of town. That's good." Kit saw the turnoff to the ranch up ahead and continued, "I wanted to have better news for Evelyn."

"I know. She worries about you."

Doubts about her ability to read people correctly nagged at her as Hawke directed his Jeep toward the house. Were her feelings for Hawke only there because of what he'd done for her concerning the Lost City of Gold and now the stalker? What would they be when her life returned to normal? She didn't want to make yet another mistake. Caution mingled with her doubts, producing uncertainty about her next step with Hawke.

All she wanted to do was escape into the bedroom and go to sleep, forget the mess her life was because of Sean. Maybe a long nap would make things look brighter after she woke up.

"When this is over with, I think you and I should talk." Hawke parked near the barn and climbed from his vehicle.

No matter what had transpired, she loved him. That wasn't going to change whether it was for the best or not. Over the Jeep's top, Kit captured his gaze and held it for a long moment, the words of doubt screaming for her to be quiet. *Wait. Think about it some more.* She gave him a nod, then started for the house.

He caught up with her halfway across the yard and took her hand. "I know today was a disappointment but—" he twisted toward her "—with some—"

A shot rang out. Kit froze as Hawke went down, letting go of her.

His eyes fluttered open. "Run. Get away," he rasped, then went limp.

"No! Not again." Without thinking, she knelt next to Hawke, holding his hand. "I love you. You can't die on me."

"Get away from him, Kit." Sean's voice boomed across the yard. She looked up to find him on the stoop with a gun pointed at Evelyn, who was gagged and bound.

"Don't make me kill her, too."

A slight squeeze told her Hawke was alive. Was he faking

it? No, blood oozed from a wound in his shoulder, right above his heart. But maybe he would be all right if she could keep Sean distracted—and somehow get Hawke some help before he bled to death.

Slowly she stood. "What do you want me to do?"

"Come here."

Each step she executed that brought her closer to the murderer underscored the danger they were all in. Fear mushroomed, and she had to fight to keep the panic at bay. Anger, helplessness, terror mingled together in Evelyn's features. She might be Evelyn's and Hawke's only hope. She couldn't let them down. Somehow she had to find a way to stop Sean.

At the stairs to the back door, Sean moved to the side to allow her to enter first. Then he pushed Evelyn forward. With her hands bound behind her, Hawke's mother was powerless, and Kit could see in her eyes the terror for her son, the same emotion rampaging through Kit.

"Tie her to the chair." Sean tossed some rope at Kit. "You'd better make sure she can't get up. I don't kill unnecessarily, but if you make it necessary, her death will be on your head."

With tears burning her eyes, Kit looped the rope around Evelyn several times before securing her with a knot her son had taught Kit. A memory of when Hawke had made her do it over and over until she'd gotten it right flashed into her mind. *If you don't, you could die if the knot slips and you fall.* His declaration to her all those weeks ago taunted her. The irony of the situation bombarded Kit with the jitters. She fumbled the piece of twine.

"I'll check your work, Kit."

Sean's warning as he hovered over her plunged her further into a sea of fright. *Please, Lord. Help.*

"I'm sorry, Evelyn." Her shaky hands stabilized enough for her to finish the task and rise.

The kindness in the woman's eyes, directed at her, bolstered Kit's vacillating courage. With the gun pointed at Hawke's mother, Sean inspected Kit's work.

"Good. I didn't realize how well you can tie knots, Kit. Holding out on me?" Sean straightened and came toward her.

Kit backed away, her gaze glued to the weapon she thought was a semiautomatic pistol. "Why are you here? What do you want?" Surprisingly her voice didn't quaver, although inside she felt as if her whole body was shaking.

"You. I just can't look out for you anymore from afar. You don't do what you're supposed to. How can I protect you when you keep associating with the wrong kind of people? Lonechief murdered his wife. Why would you want to be with him?"

"No, he didn't."

"Of course he would say that. I wouldn't expect any less. I read up on the so-called accident. You should know the ones closest to a person are always suspected first in any murder." Sean cackled, an almost hysterical noise that wasn't really anything that should be considered a laugh. "See, that's why I'm taking you away with me. You are so naive, my Kit."

She wanted to shout at him that she wasn't his anything, but that would provoke him even more. She had to get away from him and get help for Hawke.

"Where are we going?" Kit took another step back.

"A secret. You'll find out when you get there." He waved his gun toward the back door. "My car is parked behind the barn. I want to make sure that Lonechief has been taken care of—permanently."

No! Her heart beat so hard against her chest, it felt as if it was being ripped from her.

Think!

"Sean, why do you feel you have to protect me?"

"You saved my life. I'm in your debt." He nudged her forward. "Open the door. We'll have time later to talk all you want."

She followed his directions in slow motion, trying to buy Hawke an extra few minutes of life. *Lord, help.*

Out on the stoop, Kit immediately looked toward where Hawke went down. He was gone! She sidled to block Sean's view but didn't move fast enough.

"What—"

From the side, Hawke launched himself at Sean. Kit dodged to the left. The ring of a shot blasted by her ear. She spun toward the pair on the stoop locked in a struggle. Hawke pinned Sean to the concrete. They were both grappling for the pistol clutched in Sean's grasp.

What to do?

Kit glanced around for something to help Hawke. Everything was too far away. She had to act now. Hawke's movements slowed. What strength Hawke had was waning...fast. The metallic stench of his blood, now flowing freely from his wound, assailed her nostrils and prodded her into action. Both men had their grips on the weapon, Hawke trying to pry Sean's fingers loose.

Kit wedged her foot on top of Sean's arm and pressed down. Pain flitted across his face. He groaned. She stepped harder until she felt something snap under her foot. He released the pistol, and Hawke snatched it up. Grimacing, he shoved Sean off, the gun at all times pointed at his assailant.

Hawke propped himself against the clapboard. "Go call the police, Kit."

"But you're bleeding." She scrambled to his side.

"Now."

That one pain-drenched word propelled her inside where she grabbed the phone. While calling the station, she stretched the cord until she could bend down and loosen Evelyn's gag and the ropes. The woman worked one hand totally free, and Kit thrust the phone into it.

"Hawke's losing a lot of blood." Snagging a kitchen towel, Kit rushed out the back door to him.

Blessedly, he was still conscious, but the gun trembled in his hand. Sean's regard fastened onto the weapon. Although he held his arm to his chest, Sean was still a threat. She had to do something quickly. She grasped the pistol and took it from Hawke.

"Don't even think it, Sean. If you've been watching me lately, you know that Hawke has been showing me how to shoot. I won't hesitate to use it." She didn't know if that was true or not and prayed she never had to find out.

His mouth contorted in pain, Sean bristled as though he was the one wronged. "You hurt me. I just want to take care of you. He's a murderer."

A near-crazed laugh erupted from her lips. "That's a rich one." With a quick sideward glance, Kit pressed the towel into Hawke's wounded shoulder.

Sean moved slightly toward her as though readying himself to spring at her. She cocked the gun. His eyes widened, and he collapsed back against the stoop.

The back door slammed open. Evelyn hastened outside. She came to her son's side and checked him out. "It shouldn't be long before someone is here. A patrol was nearby."

While Hawke's mother went calmly about the business of taking care of her son, Kit kept her attention fully on Sean. This man would pay for all the pain he caused others.

I love you, Hawke. I love you.

But he didn't hear Kit. His eyes were closed, his face ashen, blending with the stark white of the hospital sheet pulled up over his bandaged shoulder. He'd been asleep since the doctor had left several hours ago.

Exhausted, Kit stood, needing to do something other than sit in the chair by his bed. She peered out the window of the clinic that served the pueblo. Darkness greeted her. The people of San Angelo were at home, finishing up dinner, probably unaware how close their police chief had come to being killed because of *her.*

Although Sean had been taken in by the police and his reign of terror would be over, maybe Hawke would be better off if she left now before he awakened. Look what happened to Hawke and Gregory because of her—for that matter Ronald Hoffman, too. She'd been right when she had dedicated herself to her career. She should leave now—

"Kit."

The hoarse whisper of her name told her she was too late. She would have to face Hawke and the pain she'd caused him. Slowly she pivoted toward him and took the few feet to his bedside.

"It's about time you woke up. I was just about ready to leave. You know me and food. My stomach has been rumbling…" She couldn't keep up the cheerful front as though nothing out of the ordinary had happened earlier in the afternoon. She slumped into the chair before her legs gave out.

"Hungry?"

His half grin melted her insides. A lump lodge in her throat, and all she could do was nod.

"Doc said I was gonna live, so you can quit worrying."

"Worrying? Me? I know you're too tough to let a little ole bullet stop—" The sobs came suddenly and intensely. She couldn't stop the flow of tears no matter how much she swiped at her cheeks. "I…I—"

"Kit, I'm okay. Promise." He moved to sit up and winced.

She continued to cry, everything crashing down on her. He reached for her, and she couldn't ignore the gesture. Clinging to his hand, she scooted her chair even closer to the bed and laid her head against his good arm.

Finally when the tears subsided, he said, "Did you mean what you said back at the house?"

She looked into his wonderful face. "I said a lot of things at your house."

"That you loved me?"

"Yes, but you don't have to feel—"

"Shh, Kit. I love you. I don't want to hear all the reasons we shouldn't be together. We can work out whatever we need to. I just know I don't want to live without you."

"But it's dangerous being around me."

"What would be dangerous to me is if you leave me. I might never recover."

"Hawke Lonechief…" His full-fledged smile halted her teasing words. She leaned forward and brushed her lips across his. "I guess you're stuck with me. I've caused you enough pain. I won't be responsible for any more."

"Promise?"

She answered him with a kiss.

EPILOGUE

The cool breeze of autumn blew across the mesa top. Hawke linked his fingers through Kit's and drew her closer to his side as they watched the sunrise. She snuggled into the curve of his arm.

"I'm slowly changing my mind about camping. I used to think my idea of roughing it was a two-star hotel. I think in the past five months, I've learned the true meaning of roughing it." Kit peered up at her husband of a month, his strong profile sending a warmth through her as it always did.

"I never got to ask you. Did you call Wes back yesterday?" Pulling her in front of him, her back pressing against him, Hawke kissed the top of Kit's head and rested his chin on it.

"Yeah, I finally did."

"And?"

"I listened to his apology and told him I forgave him. I know what you're thinking—that I'm a sucker for a sob story, but he's paying for his bad choices. Not too many colleges will hire him now for trying to steal my research."

He nibbled the side of her neck. "No, I wasn't thinking that. I fully expected you to forgive him. I wouldn't have xpected anything less. You've taught me so much about orgiveness and letting go."

"We learned together." She twisted around in the cage of is arms and looked up at him. "What Wes did was nothing ompared to Sean. It won't surprise me if his attorney tries claim the insanity plea for him."

"It won't work. He knew right from wrong. He needs to e locked away for the rest of his life."

"Spoken like a cop."

"Yep, and happy to be one. I feel I've finally come home." Iis embrace tightened about her.

"Speaking of home. I've been invited to another conference to speak on my discovery of the City of Gold and its npact. It's in San Francisco in November."

"I may just have to go with you on this trip. I love listenng to you talk about what we found in the cave and the ndings you and Zach made about the artifacts, especially ie gold murals."

"The best part is that the Collier/Somers Wing of the nuseum will get to display the murals first."

"No, the best part is I found you." Hawke claimed her nouth as the new day bathed them in sunlight.

* * * * *

Dear Reader,

In Forsaken Canyon, I came up with a premise that would send Kit and Hawke on an adventure. This drew them together when otherwise they wouldn't have got to know each other. The area and story is pure fiction. I used some places that were real, but most were straight out of my imagination. Like myths, though, I based my story on some facts. For example, the Southwest Indians did trade with the different groups in Mexico. Coronado did look for riches for Spain and travel all over the Southwest.

I love hearing from readers. You can contact me at:

P.O. Box 2074, Tulsa, OK 74101

or visit my Web site at www.margaretdaley.com, where you can sign up for my quarterly newsletter.

Best wishes,

Margaret Daley

QUESTIONS FOR DISCUSSION

1. Kit had a hard time giving control over to another. What are some things you've done to keep control of a situation? How did Kit have to give up control in a situation in the story? How did you learn to give up control?

2. Who is your favorite character in *Forsaken Canyon?* Why?

3. A recurring theme throughout my stories is forgiveness. It isn't always easy to do it. When have you found it difficult to forgive someone or even yourself? Did you finally? Why or why not?

4. How did Hawke deal with his guilt over Pamela? How do you deal with guilt?

5. Kit felt she had to prove herself. When she was growing up, her father made her feel unworthy of his love. She felt all she had to do was work harder, gain success and then she would be worthy. What are some of the things you've done to prove yourself to a loved one?

6. What is your favorite scene in *Forsaken Canyon?* Why?

7. When Kit faced troubles, she turned to the Lord for help. Do you turn to the Lord when life gets difficult for you? How do you depend on Him in those times?

8. Why did Kit have such a strong faith? How did it affect how she lived?

9. How did Hawke learn to put his past behind him and live a fulfilled life?

10. Have you ever been driven to do something as Kit was in trying to prove her theory? She took risks and pushed herself to do things she normally wouldn't. Did you accomplish your goal? Why or why not?

11. How did Hawke deal with his wife's death? What are some of the things you've done to deal with a death of a loved one?

12. Having a stalker would be scary. Have you ever dealt with a stalker or someone who wouldn't leave you alone? What did you do? How would you have handled Kit's situation with the stalker?

REQUEST YOUR FREE BOOKS!

2 FREE RIVETING INSPIRATIONAL NOVELS
PLUS 2 FREE MYSTERY GIFTS

Love Inspired® SUSPENSE

YES! Please send me 2 FREE Love Inspired® Suspense novels and my 2 FREE mystery gifts (gifts are worth about $10). After receiving them, if I don't wish to receive any more books, I can return the shipping statement marked "cancel". If I don't cancel, I will receive 4 brand-new novels every month and be billed just $4.24 per book in the U.S. or $4.74 per book in Canada, plus 25¢ shipping and handling per book and applicable taxes, if any*. That's a savings of over 20% off the cover price! I understand that accepting the 2 free books and gifts places me under no obligation to buy anything. I can always return a shipment and cancel at any time. Even if I never buy another book, the two free books and gifts are mine to keep forever.   123 IDN ERXX 323 IDN ERXM

_____
Name   (PLEASE PRINT)

_____
Address   Apt. #

_____
City   State/Prov.   Zip/Postal Code

_____
Signature (if under 18, a parent or guardian must sign)

Order online at www.LoveInspiredSuspense.com
Or mail to Steeple Hill Reader Service:

IN U.S.A.: P.O. Box 1867, Buffalo, NY 14240-1867
IN CANADA: P.O. Box 609, Fort Erie, Ontario L2A 5X3

Not valid to current subscribers of Love Inspired Suspense books.

Want to try two free books from another series?
Call 1-800-873-8635 or visit www.morefreebooks.com

* Terms and prices subject to change without notice. N.Y. residents add applicable sales tax. Canadian residents will be charged applicable provincial taxes and GST. Offer not valid in Quebec. This offer is limited to one order per household. All orders subject to approval. Credit or debit balances in a customer's account(s) may be offset by any other outstanding balance owed by or to the customer. Please allow 4 to 6 weeks for delivery. Offer available while quantities last.

Your Privacy: Steeple Hill Books is committed to protecting your privacy. Our Privacy Policy is available online at www.SteepleHill.com or upon request from the Reader Service. From time to time we make our lists of customers available to reputable third parties who may have a product or service of interest to you. If you would prefer we not share your name and address, please check here. ☐

LISUS08R

Widower and former soldier Evan Paterson invites his five-year-old daughter's best friend and her friend's single mother to the ranch for the holiday meal. Can these two pint-sized matchmakers show two stubborn grownups what being thankful truly means, and help them learn how to forgive and love again?

Look for

A Texas Thanksgiving

by

Margaret Daley

Available November 2008 wherever books are sold.

Steeple
Hill®

Love Inspired ®
SUSPENSE

TITLES AVAILABLE NEXT MONTH

Don't miss these four stories in November

THE GOOD NEIGHBOR by Sharon Mignerey
Detective Wade Prescott has his prime suspect:
Megan Burke. He found her in the yard beside the
body of her neighbor's grandson, didn't he? Case closed.
Yet Megan's sweet demeanor has Wade believing
in her innocence. And if she is innocent, a murderer
is still at large....

THE PROTECTOR'S PROMISE by Shirlee McCoy
The Sinclair Brothers

Who could be after his widowed neighbor and
her little girl? Grayson Sinclair vows to find out—*without*
getting emotionally involved. He won't let anyone hurt
Honor Malone, or her daughter. But the threat is closer to
home than anyone realizes.

SHIELD OF REFUGE by Carol Steward
In the Line of Fire

No evidence, no other witnesses—no wonder Officer
Garrett Matthews doubts Amber Scott's claims that
she saw a kidnapping. Then someone begins tailing Amber,
and Garrett starts to suspect that she's telling the truth.
And that means that the danger she's in is real.

HOLIDAY ILLUSION by Lynette Eason
Little Paulo desperately needs a new heart. But for the
surgery, orphanage director Anna Freeman must take him
to the city she fled in fear years ago. And she finally has to
tell Dr. Lucas Freeman about her secrets. Her past. And the
danger stalking them all.

LISCNM1008